"Do you want to get married?" Kacey asked.

"Uh." Her eyes widened. "I'm not dating anyone, so I can't get married."

Good save, Delta. He picked up his mug of coffee and took a sip.

"I thought you were dating Daddy."

Garrett began to choke.

"Are you all right?" Delta smacked him on the back.

He continued to cough for another minute before waggling his finger at Kacey. "Delta and I are just friends."

"But you bought her that gift."

"That wasn't a gift," Delta corrected. "The shoeing stall is for work."

"And you were hugging before."

Garrett didn't blame his daughter for being confused. Between dinner at Harlan's and everything else she'd w̶i̶t̶ d a bit of trouble di̶s̶t̶i̶ ̶ sn't where Delta was

WRANGLING CUPID'S COWBOY

BY
AMANDA RENEE

This book is produced from independently certified FSC™ paper to ensure responsible forest management.

For more information visit: www.harpercollins.co.uk/green

Printed and bound in Spain
by Blackprint

MILLS & BOON

First Published in Great Britain 2018
By Mills & Boon, an imprint of HarperCollins*Publishers*
1 London Bridge Street, London, SE1 9GF

© 2018 Amanda Renee

ISBN: 978-0-263-93640-7

23-0118

Amanda Renee was raised in the Northeast and now wriggles her toes in the warm coastal Carolina sands. Her career began when she was discovered through Harlequin's So You Think You Can Write contest. When not creating stories about love and laughter, she enjoys the company of her schnoodle—Duffy—camping, playing guitar and piano, photography and anything involving animals. You can visit her at www.amandarenee.com.

For my superagent,
Pamela Harty of The Knight Agency.

Thank you for your unwavering faith,
support and guidance.

Chapter One

"I know women love shoes, but isn't this taking it a little too far?"

Delta lowered a freshly shod horse's hoof to the ground and straightened to acknowledge the lame wise-crack. She half expected to find a cocksure ranch hand looking to score. Instead, a rugged cowboy with deep maple-brown eyes and hair to match rested casually against the work truck she'd parked in the Silver Bells Ranch's wide stable entrance.

"Garrett Slade." He took a step toward her and extended his hand. "I'm the ranch's new partner. My brother Dylan has told me you're the best farrier in the state. It's a pleasure to meet you."

"Delta Grace." His muscular fingers encircled her palm, sending a tingle down to the tips of her toes. "Dylan's much too kind, but I appreciate it just the same. And the pleasure is all mine," she drawled. Delta inwardly cringed at the unfamiliar licentious tone she had never heard come out of her mouth. He was the most attractive man she'd laid eyes on since heaven knew when, and she found it most unsettling.

She stepped around Garrett and gave the draft

horse's bristly muzzle a rub. The animal inquisitively nudged the pocket of her pink-and-black plaid flannel shirt until she unbuttoned it and rewarded him with the baby carrots she had tucked away earlier. She returned to her truck and packed up her tools before removing her heavyweight apron chaps under the heat of Garrett's gaze. "I'm finished here for the day, but I'll need to return tomorrow for Lightning Bug, the quarter horse with navicular disease. I need to be here when Dr. Presley radiographs the hoof so we can discuss further shoeing modifications. He's improved significantly since the early fall when Jax first noticed it."

A flicker of sadness crossed his features at the mention of Garrett's uncle, who had died six weeks earlier. They were almost halfway through January and the ranch's future precariously balanced on the newly formed partnership between the two Slade brothers. They had managed to avoid foreclosure on the 730-acre guest ranch, but they still had major renovations to undertake for them to profitably compete with the more modern ranches cropping up around them.

"I am truly sorry for your loss. Jax was a great man."

Garrett nodded wordlessly and led the Belgian horse to his stall. Delta secured the side compartment of her truck while trying to ignore the way his fawn-colored barn coat framed his broad shoulders. If the Silver Bells Ranch wasn't her largest account, she would have asked him to join her for a drink in Jax's memory. But she wasn't willing to cross that line under any circumstances.

Delta firmly believed her professional and personal life should remain independent of each other. She'd successfully maintained that balance back in Missoula, but it proved more difficult since she had moved to Saddle Ridge in northwestern Montana. A town forty times smaller meant running into customers no matter where she went. Lucky for her, Missoula was a two-hour straight shot south and she visited her family and friends whenever she wanted.

She had a few single girlfriends in town, but Liv was pregnant with triplets and Maddie was so in love with the baby thing she spent all her free time helping Liv prepare for their arrival. Weeknights had become lonely and it didn't help that Saddle Ridge had already gone head over boots for Valentine's Day. She never understood the fervent commercialization of the blasted holiday. Back home she could escape it. Not in Saddle Ridge. Everywhere she turned, there was another cupid aiming an arrow at her heart. She'd like to shove that arrow somewh—

"I wanted to discuss a few things if you have the time to spare." Garrett's voice shattered her mental assault on the chubby cherub.

"Sure. Silver Bells was my last stop today." Delta folded her arms tight across her chest as a bitter wind blew into the stables. "Just let me move my truck out of your entrance." Minutes later, she was back inside as Garrett slid the tall wooden doors shut behind her. The cold lingered on her body, causing her to regret leaving her jacket on the front seat.

"Let's talk in my office where it's warmer."

His office? Delta found it interesting that Dylan had handed over the responsibility of the horses to Garrett. They had been his greatest pride, but she understood the necessity to move into his uncle's position of managing the ranch along with the lodge and staff.

Snorts and nickers coupled with the lone scrape of a shovel against a stall floor masked the awkward silence that grew between them as she followed him down the center corridor. The friendliness that had transpired between them only moments ago seemed to fade with each stride.

The office door creaked as Garrett opened it for her to enter. Fluorescent lights swathed the large room with the flick of a switch. She had been there before, but it had resembled more of a cozy den. Not anymore. A row of chest-high filing cabinets with shelves above them replaced the oversize leather couch along the rough wood wall opposite the desk. And the kitchenette now consisted of a coffeepot and nothing more. Dylan had faithfully stocked boxes of cookies, chips and other nibbles for his employees to snack on during the day. It appeared those were a thing of the past, too.

"Have a seat." Garrett removed his hat and hung it on the freestanding rack behind his desk before shrugging off his coat and hanging it on the other side. He waited for her to sit in the chair across from him before doing the same. "I'm not sure how much you know about the changes the ranch is undergoing, but I'd like to discuss a few cost-saving ideas with you."

"Okay." Cost-saving automatically registered as less compensation in her brain.

"I've only been here a week, so I haven't had the chance to review all the stables expenses, but I have seen a handful of your invoices." Garrett fanned out five of her itemized bills across the worn black walnut surface. "Our farrier costs seem high."

"You have almost a hundred horses. Thirty of which are Belgians. And you have to factor in all the therapeutic shoeing, too." Delta hadn't known what to expect from their conversation, but this wasn't a good start. "I realize it's none of my concern, but since we're on the subject, I don't understand why you're maintaining this many horses when you don't have the business to support them any longer."

"Because Dylan doesn't want to thin the stables. I've agreed to give the ranch six months before revisiting the idea." Garrett removed a pad from the top drawer and scanned his neatly written notes. "In the meantime, I need to reduce the ranch's overhead at once so we can balance their expense. Please don't think you're my only target. But since you're here today, I'd like to tackle this expense first. Had Dylan or Jax discussed cold-shoeing with you? The cost is significantly lower."

Target? Tackle? They weren't playing a sport. She was a fourth-generation farrier and she took her job seriously.

"The quality is lower, as well." Delta only cold-shod a horse when the animal had an intolerance to the hiss of firing up a forge or the smoke produced when a hot shoe met the hoof. "It's much easier to hammer and shape a hot shoe than file a cold one and it provides a more exacting fit. In my opinion, cold-shoeing is done by less experienced farriers. Some do exceptional work, but they're not equipped to handle the corrective or specialized work I do for your horses. As you've already said, your brother considers me the top in the state."

She'd had to justify her prices in the past, but Delta hadn't anticipated having to defend her value, as well.

"I think we're getting off on the wrong foot, no pun intended." Garrett gathered her invoices and stacked them in front of him. "I'm not looking to replace you as Silver Bells' farrier. I'm asking if we can cold-shoe from this point forward and hot-shoe only when necessary."

Delta weighed her options carefully. Just as Garrett had said, cold-shoeing was significantly cheaper. It also forced her to do twice, if not three times, as many jobs to offset the difference.

"I prefer not to, but you're the customer. If you want cold-shoeing, then that's what I will do."

"You are capable of cold-shoeing, right?"

"I beg your pardon." Delta abruptly stood, inadvertently shoving her chair backward into a filing cabinet. "I assure you I'm more than capable of any shoeing requirements you might have. But I will also assure you, I'm the only farrier around that will work on your Belgians."

"Why is that?" Garrett asked, without a single muscle in his body reacting to her outburst.

"Because they're obstinate and they weren't trained from the beginning to lift their feet. The ones that do tend to lean on me. Since Silver Bells doesn't have a proper shoeing stall where I can secure their foot to work on it, my back takes a beating."

"Good to know." He jotted down a note.

"If that's all, I have another appointment to get to."

"I thought you said this was your last stop of the day," Garrett challenged.

"I was mistaken. I have one more to make." Delta

had an imminent date with a bar stool after this conversation. She marched to the door and willed herself to open it nicely. "See you tomorrow."

"I'm looking forward to it," Garrett called after her as she stormed toward the exit.

"I'm not," Delta mumbled to herself. She hated when a perfectly good man went from sexy to infuriating in a matter of minutes. It was a waste of nice-fitting Wranglers.

THE SOUND OF Delta's boots reverberated against the floor as she barreled out of the stables. Garrett had hoped she would have been more sympathetic to the ranch's difficult financial position. And maybe she already was. He didn't know enough about her to say one way or the other. But a small part of him wanted to know a lot more about the mahogany-haired beauty that couldn't get away from him fast enough.

According to Dylan, Delta had extended their payment terms out to ninety days from her usual fifteen. That alone had been generous, but it still wasn't enough to help their bottom line. Now here he was, a total stranger, asking her to take more of a financial hit for him.

He respected Delta's need to earn a living. Hell, he could even understand her getting upset at the prospect of less money. Her attitude was a bit much, though. Answering his questions was part of the job, and she shouldn't have been insulted by them or his request.

Back in Wyoming, his farrier had cold-shod their horses to his satisfaction. So then why did he have a strong desire to call Delta and apologize? He had done nothing wrong. He just wished he hadn't made her mad. Although making people mad seemed to be his new norm.

His in-laws were mad at him for moving their grand-kids thirteen hours away from Wheatland, Wyoming, back to his hometown of Saddle Ridge, Montana, with only two days' notice. Garrett had been living with his in-laws and managing their three-thousand-acre cattle ranch for the last three years, after his wife had passed away from pancreatic cancer. He'd known for a while it was time for him and the kids to stand on their own, but he didn't know how or where.

When Dylan offered him a chance to partner with him on the Silver Bells Guest Ranch, he hadn't had to think twice. They weren't quite on their own, but he needed to be near his own family again. Plus, Garrett's brother-in-law had been more than ready to take over the cattle ranch and he was confident he'd left it in ca-pable hands. Moving back to town was the best choice for him and his kids. If only his seven-year-old daugh-ter felt the same way.

Kacey was mad at him. He had torn her from her friends and grandparents during Christmas vacation and then told her they were moving a few days later. She had cried all night after her first day of school al-most two weeks ago. The crying had stopped, but she no longer spoke to him. The silent treatment was alive and well in the Slade household. Except for his four-year-old son, Bryce. The kid found happiness every-where and loved his new preschool.

Garrett fired up the snowmobile and headed for the ranch's main entrance. Even the biting wind against his cheeks didn't help erase the flash of Delta's bright smile when they first met...or her resentment toward him when she left. She was the last person he needed to be thinking about. His kids were his first priority, the ranch second. There was no room for hurt feelings.

He arrived at the front gate and waited. The school bus would drop Kacey off in a few minutes and he hoped a ride to the house would cheer her up. The scowl on his daughter's face when the bus doors opened told him that wouldn't be the case. He needed to stick to horses. At least they liked him.

"Get on, baby," Garrett said as she marched past him. "It's too cold to walk."

"You're embarrassing me in front of the other kids," Kacey ground out. She gripped the straps of her backpack tighter and trudged down the ranch road. "Now they're going to pick on me tomorrow."

"No they won't." Garrett wondered if all girls were this dramatic at her age. "Get on. The bus left and I'm not taking no for an answer." He scooted back for her to sit in front of him.

"What about my bag?"

"Give it to me." Garrett lengthened the straps on the yellow *Beauty and the Beast* backpack and slung it over his shoulder. Appropriate considering he felt like the Beast this afternoon. "Now get on."

Kacey climbed over his legs, doing her best not to hold on to him for support. Garrett grinned and revved the engine, causing the snowmobile to lurch forward a few inches. She immediately leaned against him and gripped his arms. "And away we go."

Dylan hopped out of his lifted black pickup before

helping Bryce down as Garrett drove up to the small two-bedroom log cabin. It had been Dylan's until he'd moved into their uncle's house. Garrett had given each of the kids a bedroom and he'd taken the loft. It served his needs, plus it wasn't like he was bringing anyone home to share his bed. He doubted he'd ever be ready for that again. Rebecca had been his entire world for nine years until Kacey came along. And then Bryce. His family had been perfect.

The second the snowmobile stopped, Kacey slid out from under his arms and stomped up the front porch steps. He was getting tired of seeing the back of his daughter's head all the time.

"Daddy!" Bryce ran to him. "I can write my name."

Garrett lifted him into his arms. "You can? You'll have to show me when we get inside."

"Hey, man, I like the new look." Dylan nodded to the backpack. "Kind of clashes with your jacket, but I think you wear it well."

"I thought it complemented my eyes." Garrett laughed as he climbed the stairs. "Thanks for picking up Bryce from preschool. I appreciate it."

"No problem." Dylan followed him into the house, just in time to hear Kacey slam her bedroom door. "It gives me a chance to prepare myself for when Holly's this age."

"I think you have a while considering she's only a few weeks old."

"You and Harlan keep telling me they grow up fast." Dylan glanced down the hall toward Kacey's room. "I take it there hasn't been any improvement."

Garrett set Bryce down and helped him out of his

snow boots and jacket. "I made it worse. I embarrassed her in front of the kids on the bus because I picked her up on a snowmobile." He eased Kacey's backpack from his shoulders and tossed it on the armchair. "My kid hates me."

"Has she really said that?"

"No, but she thinks it." Garrett kicked off his own boots.

"I can remember us hating Mom and Dad a time or two when we were kids. It's growing pains and the stress of starting over in a new place while trying to make friends. We were lucky. We went to school with the same kids year after year. You and I don't have a clue how hard it is for her to adjust."

"I know you're right. It's just difficult to take sometimes. I hate knowing she's hurting. She barely eats and stays locked in her room." Garrett grabbed a box of crayons and a stack of paper from the kitchen counter and set them on the coffee table. "Show me what you learned in school today, champ."

Bryce chose a blue crayon and began drawing a large letter *B*. His tiny tongue stuck out between his teeth as he concentrated on his letters.

"How did things go with Delta this afternoon?" Dylan sat cross-legged on the floor across from Bryce. "That's the most perfect *B* I've ever seen."

"She's mad at me, too." And that bothered him more than it should. He peered over Bryce's shoulder as he drew a *C*. "Very good, you're almost there."

Dylan's brows rose. "You better not run off my farrier. She's one of the nicest people I've met. She stays mostly to herself, but she's a real sweetheart."

"Look, Daddy." Bryce handed Garrett the paper.

"Wow!" He ran his fingers over the printed letters. "I'm so proud of you." He gave Bryce a hug and held it up proudly for Dylan to see. "My son did that."

"Way to go, little man." Dylan high-fived the boy.

"Can I go show Kacey?" Bryce asked.

"We'll show her when she's feeling better. Go hang it on the refrigerator for me while I talk to your uncle Dylan for a minute." His son's sock-covered feet thumped across the hardwood floor as he ran from the room. "The farrier bills are astronomical. With you wanting to keep the horses, I had to cut costs. So, I asked her to cold-shoe them from now on."

"No wonder she was mad." Dylan eased off the floor and onto a chair. "That's not her style. She hasn't been able to take on new customers in months. She's in high demand because of her superior craftsmanship. I like her work. Her knowledge has prevented a lot of problems. When our last farrier retired, she effortlessly slid into the position. Let her do her job the way she sees fit."

Garrett sagged against the back of the couch. "If you wanted a silent partner, then you should have said so ahead of time."

"I didn't say that."

"You asked me to go in fifty-fifty and that's what I did. My fifty percent needs to cut costs in those stables, but you're making it impossible. I can't sell any horses. I can't ask the farrier to save us money. You told me last week you're happy with our feed distributor. What's left? The veterinarian?"

"Don't you dare." Dylan braced his hands on his

knees. "Lydia Presley knows each of my horses by name."

"Our horses," Garrett corrected. "A partnership shouldn't be difficult to grasp considering you had one with Jax."

"I accept our partnership, but I need you to focus on moving forward and making us money. I cut back all I could last year. When I asked you to run the stables, I didn't mean for you to change anything. We have guests booked into the ranch the first of the month and we need to stick to our renovation schedule. Let's try to avoid any further hiccups, please. I've had enough of those around here."

"Fine." Now Garrett needed to apologize to Delta tomorrow. He'd spent twenty minutes around the woman and already made an ass of himself. Not that he should care. The ranch employed her services and that was the extent of their relationship. "I need to feed my kids. At least the one that will eat." He started for the kitchen and tripped over Bryce's boots, causing him to stub his toe on the fireplace hearth. Totally his fault. He'd left them there. "Dammit, that hurts."

"I have an idea." Dylan slapped him on the back. "I'll take the kids to my house, feed them and help Kacey with her homework. You need to let off some steam tonight and Kacey would probably enjoy spending time with Holly. Go into town, get a drink and a bite to eat and then pick them up when you're ready."

It was the best idea he'd heard all week. He needed to clear his head of the ranch, and that included Delta.

The woman had already stuck in his mind like a fly to honey, and he didn't need any more complications in his life.

Chapter Two

Complication must be Garrett's middle name. No sooner
had he walked through the doors of the Iron Horse Bar
& Grill, when he spotted Delta at the far end of the
dimly lit bar. Alone. Apparently, her next stop hadn't
been a customer.

Garrett weighed his options. Walk out before she saw
him, grab a booth in the back and pretend he never noticed her, or eat crow and get it over with. Delta's gaze
met his as she lifted a drink to her lips and froze. He
could have sworn her shoulders sagged at the recognition, but between the neon beer sign behind her and the
waitress temporarily blocking his view as she swept
under the stools, he wasn't a hundred percent certain.
Delta lowered her glass and shook her head, destroy-
ing any illusion of subtlety, and then waved him over.
Garrett had hoped for a burger and a beer, but it looked
like he was eating crow for an appetizer. So much for
unwinding.

Johnny Cash's "Ring of Fire" played on the jukebox as he crossed the room and he couldn't help but
notice his boots hit the floor in time with the beat. Before Kacey was born, he and Rebecca had spent every

Friday and Saturday night dancing around this very floor. He hadn't expected the memory to be so vivid eight years later.

"I hope our conversation earlier didn't drive you here." Garrett pulled out the corner bar stool next to hers and sat down. "It's not even five o'clock."

"I could say the same to you." Delta sipped at her drink. "I was hungry, frustrated and this is the only place in town that's not decked out for Valentine's Day." Her face soured at the mention of the holiday.

"Bad breakup?" he asked.

"Something like that," she mumbled, staring down at the amber liquid as she swirled it in the glass.

"I hear you." Garrett motioned for the bartender. "It's not my favorite either." His wife had died four days before the holiday, reminding him every year of what he'd lost.

"Bad breakup for you, too?"

"Something like that." If only it had been a breakup, maybe his heart would have survived.

Delta nudged a platter of nachos toward him. "Help yourself. I can't eat all this on top of the sandwich I ordered."

"Thanks." Garrett took her cordiality as a positive sign and reached for a few of the neatly stacked napkins along the back edge of the bar.

"What can I get you?" the bartender asked.

"I'll have whatever she's drinking."

One of Delta's brows rose. "Brave man."

"Why's that?" Garrett couldn't help noticing how naturally beautiful she was without a lick of makeup. Truth was, he'd noticed it the moment he first saw her, but he forced it to the back of his mind. He had no business admiring anyone the ranch conducted business with. It was unprofessional and he wasn't interested in anything more.

"I'm drinking chipotle whiskey." Her mischievous smile presented more of a dare than a warning. "I don't know if you can handle it."

"I'm sure I can handle it. I'm a man. We're rugged." Garrett hooked his boots on the stool's footrest and followed Delta's eyes to the television she remained transfixed upon…sports scores from last night's games.

"If you say so," she said, her attention still unwavering from the screen.

"Seriously?" If Dylan thought Delta was one of the nicest people he had ever met, his brother needed to get out more. "I guess I gave you some first impression, huh?"

"Listen, don't get me wrong. I get it." Delta leveled her gaze to his. "You're trying to save money wherever you can. But are you aware I had started charging your uncle twenty percent less than all my other customers over a year ago to help ease some of the ranch's financial burden? Then I extended your payment terms six months later. I've taken two significant hits from my largest customer and now I'm taking another one. I won't lie to you. It hurts. But, I shouldn't have acted or reacted the way I did."

Well, if that hadn't made him feel like more of a jerk he didn't know what would. "I knew about the payment terms, which I hope to amend sooner rather than later, but I had no idea about the discount. I should be the one apologizing. I was a bit overenthusiastic earlier."

"Just a bit." Delta's smile tightened.

The bartender set Garrett's drink on the bar top. "Did you want to place a food order?"

Garrett looked over the glossy double-sided menu. "Bacon cheeseburger, medium rare with fries."

"Sure thing." The man turned to Delta. "Your order's almost up. Do you want them to hold it and serve it with his or bring it out when it's ready?"

"Please don't wait on my account." Garrett had ruined enough of her day. He didn't want to add dinner to it.

"I still haven't made a dent in these nachos." Delta sighed down at the plate. "Go ahead and hold mine."

"You didn't have to do that."

"Yeah, well, I can't sit here and eat with you watching me."

"I could leave."

"You could, but that would be rude of me to ask. Besides, I ordered a turkey club. It's not like it's going to get cold." Delta nudged the nachos closer to him. "Please help me eat these."

Garrett lifted a heavily topped tortilla chip. "Think we can start over?" he asked before popping the gooey piece of heaven into his mouth. "Man, these are awesome. You never used to be able to get nachos here. A basket of chips and salsa was about all you could order outside of a burger or a bar pie."

"Been away for a while?"

"Almost five years. I visited my brothers when I could, but it's been even longer since I came in here." Garrett lifted his drink. "You still haven't answered me about starting over."

"Hard to forget being asked to do my job differently."

"We'll forget about that, too. Fresh start. This is our first meeting, and you can go back to doing what you do best."

"I'm not even going to question why you changed your mind, but I'll take the do-over." Delta raised her glass to his. "It's a pleasure to meet you, Garrett Slade."

"Same here." Garrett's eyes had already begun to water from the scent of the whiskey, but he took a man-sized swallow anyway. "Good Lord, woman!" He exhaled slowly, surprised that flames didn't shoot out of his mouth. "How do you drink this stuff?"

Delta's impish laugh rose above the music. "I can take the heat."

Garrett froze. He hadn't heard those five words in years. He squeezed his eyes shut against the memory, wishing he'd chosen someplace other than the Iron Horse tonight.

"Are you all right?" Delta's warm hand upon his arm snapped him back to the present. "You need to take it easy with that stuff. It's meant to be sipped, not chugged."

Garrett shook his head. "It's not that." The concern reflecting in Delta's caramel-brown eyes touched his soul in a way he hadn't thought possible again. "This is the first time I've been here without my wife. We practically lived in this place before we moved to Wyoming."

"Where is she now?"

"She died." He took another sip of his drink, needing the heat to numb the pain of the memory. "Pancreatic cancer."

Delta's grasp tightened. He could have sworn he

heard her swallow hard at the revelation, but when he lifted his gaze to hers, only sympathy greeted him in return.

She eased her grip. "Her loss must have been devastating for you."

"Thank you." Garrett patted her hand and shifted on his stool, effectively breaking all physical contact between them. He stared down at the gold band he hadn't found the will to remove. In his heart, Rebecca would always be his wife. There could never be anyone else. "You reminded me of her when you said you could take the heat. Rebecca used to say those exact same words."

"Really? Wow." Delta rubbed her hands up and down her jean-clad thighs.

"Chemotherapy killed her taste buds and she constantly bet that she could out heat me."

Delta stilled. "I've heard that."

"Some things just stick in your mind, you know?" He folded his napkin into a tiny triangle. "It's been almost three years and sometimes it feels like yesterday. Coming here is just hitting me harder than I expected."

"I can imagine." She picked up a chip and broke it in half before setting it back down on the platter. "So, this was your spot, huh?" Sadness reflected in her eyes as she spoke.

"Up until the day we moved away." Garrett straightened his shoulders. "But enough about that. Tell me about yourself. I don't remember you when I was growing up here, although you're definitely younger than me."

"I'm from Missoula, born and raised." She cracked

a knuckle against her glass. "And I'm thirty, so if I'm younger, it isn't by much."

"I have three years on you." Garrett watched the kitchen door, hoping their orders would come out soon. He already felt he had said too much. "So…what brought you to Saddle Ridge?"

"Henry, Silver Bells' former farrier. I don't know how well you knew him."

"We spoke a few times in passing. Dylan and Jax always talked about him, though. Seems like a good guy from what I've heard."

"He and my dad apprenticed together way back in the day." Delta swiveled slightly to face him, causing her knee to brush against his. "Oh, I'm sorry. I didn't mean to bump you." Her hand rested lightly on his leg for a brief second, but it was long enough to send his blood coursing quicker through his veins. "When Henry decided to retire, he called and asked if I was interested in taking over his customers. Before that, I was working for my dad. Coming here gave me a chance to have my own business. And Missoula is still close enough for me to visit my family on weekends and holidays."

Garrett tried focusing on her face as a whole, but he kept wandering down to her mouth as she spoke. Her lips were full and naturally darkened, as if she'd just been kissed. Not that he needed to be thinking about kissing Delta or anyone else. His heart was permanently shuttered. *Stick to the topic, Garrett.* "How long have you been here?"

"A little over a year." She sipped her whiskey with ease. "Where were you in Wyoming?"

"Wheatland." Garrett rolled the glass slowly in the

palms of his hands. Oddly enough, he found the liquor less intoxicating than Delta. "My wife and I moved there almost five years ago to be closer to her parents. I managed their cattle ranch up until a few weeks ago."

A waitress set both of their meals in front of them. She was one more person he didn't recognize. It used to be he knew everyone and their brother. When did he become a stranger in his own hometown? At least he'd made one new friend tonight.

"Silver Bells must be a big change from a cattle ranch."

"It is." Garrett took a bite of his burger and nodded. "It was time, though. I love my wife's family, but we were living with them. I appreciated their help with the kids, but the place had a shroud of grief hanging over it. They talked about Rebecca all the time and her mother still set a place for her at the table." Garrett didn't even have to close his eyes to envision that empty seat across from him. It made every meal almost unbearable. "My kids are mad because I refuse to do that here, but I don't want them growing up in a constant state of depression. That's not to say I love Rebecca any less." His voice began to rise. "She'll always be my wife. No one will ever replace her."

Delta reared back at the declaration as if he had physically shoved her. The force of his words had startled even him.

"I can't imagine anyone would try." She inched away from him and turned her attention to her sandwich.

"I'm sorry. You're the first woman I've really sat down and spoken with outside of family. Apparently I left my manners back in Wyoming."

"Let me make this easy for you." Delta side-glanced him. "I'm just one of the guys where you're concerned. I can assure you it will never be anything more. I'm assuming you're okay with that."

"Suits me just fine." Then why did her matter-of-fact attitude on the subject sit on his chest like a bobcat on a briar bush? He certainly wasn't interested in her.

"Good. Now that that's out of the way...how old are your children?"

"Bryce is four and Kacey will be eight next month. Rebecca died just before her fifth birthday and she hasn't wanted to celebrate since. I'm hoping this year will be different. And I need to stop running on about myself and my problems." Garrett ordered a beer before returning his attention to Delta. "I've monopolized the entire conversation."

Delta dabbed her mouth with a napkin. "We all need a friendly ear sometimes."

"At least I've wandered into the friend zone and out of enemy range."

"Friends, huh?"

Her bemused expression gave him pause. "It's a start, at least."

"I'll give you that much."

Over the rest of their meal Garrett continued to tell her about his kids. She'd listened intently as he spoke and had carried on their conversation as if he hadn't made a repeated ass out of himself earlier. By the time their plates were empty, he realized he hadn't asked much about her. Guilt over Rebecca forced him to tamp down the desire to make plans to have dinner with Delta again. Tonight was a one-time deal stemming from a chance encounter. That was it.

"Buy you another round?" The question was out of his mouth before he could stop it.

Delta rose from her stool, tugged a few bills from the pocket of her jeans and tossed them on the bar. "Thank you, but I need to get going. Jake's waiting for me."

Jake? "Oh, okay. At least allow me to pay for your dinner to make up for this afternoon."

"Nah, I got it. Besides, I thought we just met tonight." Delta winked. "I'll see you tomorrow when we meet with Dr. Presley." She began to walk away and then turned toward him. "Welcome home, Garrett. I hope you find the peace you're looking for."

BY THE TIME he arrived at Dylan's to pick up Kacey and Bryce, he felt more certain moving back to Saddle Ridge had been the right decision for him and his family. He could hear his kids from the great room as he climbed the steps of the log cabin's front porch. Peering in the window, he saw Kacey dancing around the room with his brother while Bryce and Emma—Dylan's fiancée—clapped along with the music. It had been a long time since he'd heard his daughter laugh so freely. And it was better than any song playing on a honky-tonk jukebox.

Dylan caught his reflection in the window and waved him inside.

"Daddy we had pasketti!" Bryce ran over to him.

"Spaghetti," Kacey corrected. "You're old enough to say it right."

Wise beyond her years, his daughter still hadn't relinquished playing mother to her brother. She'd taken on the role herself the moment he and Rebecca told Kacey she was sick. In hindsight, they never should have told her. She'd barely had a chance to be a child.

"I see that." Garrett knelt on the floor next to his son. He tried to give his daughter a hug, but she slipped under his arm and sat next to Emma on the couch. He didn't want to pressure Kacey, but damned if it didn't kill him to see her happy up until the moment he walked in the room. "Looks like you wore most of your pasketti, little man."

Kacey huffed at him. "You're not helping, Dad."

"He refused to wear a bib." Emma frowned. "Or a towel or a napkin. I wanted to get him changed and wash his shirt before you got back, but I didn't have anything that would fit him."

"It's no big deal. He's always been a messy eater. I keep hoping he'll grow out of it soon."

"How was dinner?" Dylan asked.

"Good. I ran into Delta at the Iron Horse. And don't worry. I apologized and told her she can continue to do her job as she sees fit."

"Thank God for that."

"We wound up having dinner together although I'm afraid I did most of the talking. She seems pretty nice."

"Dinner together, huh? You sly dog." Dylan nudged his arm. "You went on a date with Delta."

Garrett put a finger to his lips and glanced over at his daughter, who continued to ignore him. "Please," he whispered. "Kacey's mad at me enough. And I have absolutely zero interest in pursuing anything with Delta. It was just two people sharing a meal."

"Okay, okay." Dylan held up his hands in surrender.

"One question, though. When she left, she said Jake was waiting for her. Who's Jake?"

"He wasn't with her today?"

"No." Garrett hadn't spent much time with Delta in the stables, but as far as he knew, she was there alone. "Does he work for her?"

"Work for her? No." His brother laughed. "They, um, live together. I'm sure you'll meet him soon. When you see one, you usually see the other. Why the curiosity about Jake if there's nothing between you and Delta?"

"Just wondering." He hadn't expected her to have a boyfriend after her comment about Valentine's Day. Garrett lowered Bryce to the floor. "Run and get your stuff together. I need to get you home and into a bath, then it's off to bed." He tried to shake the flip-floppy sensation growing inside him. He was fine two seconds ago. It had to be from the chipotle whiskey. "Kacey, honey, time to go." Garrett gave Emma a hug as she stood up from the couch. "Thank you for entertaining them tonight. I really appreciate it. I know you have your hands full with Holly."

"Holly's been a dream baby so far." Emma held Garrett's face between her palms and smiled up at him. "I know this move hasn't been easy on you or the kids. They're welcome here anytime. Don't you ever think twice about it."

Garrett took her hands in his and gave them a gentle squeeze. "My brother struck gold with you. He's a lucky man."

"Holly and I are the lucky ones. We inherited an amazing family."

"Enough already," Dylan called out from the kitchen table. "I swear you two are the ones who are related. I've never seen two more sentimental people in my entire life. Emma still has the baby hormone thing going on, but you, dear brother..." Dylan's head tilted questioningly. "That must have been some dinner."

Garrett ignored his brother's comment and walked out to bundle the kids into the car. He'd been feeling nostalgic ever since Christmas when he first came home. He had so many memories in this town. Most good. One life-shattering.

He still hadn't been able to drive past their old family ranch. The place where their father had died at the hands of their brother, Ryder. Shortly after the funeral, their mother sold the ranch and moved to California where she remarried and rebuilt her life. He and Rebecca had left from Saddle Ridge to escape the pain of the past, and years later he'd come back to escape even more pain. His grief emotionally drained him every day. He had to work—to continually stay active to keep his mind occupied and remain strong for his children. He refused to let them down.

Tonight, despite the bittersweet memories of Rebecca, some of the weight had lifted from his shoulders. He'd enjoyed taking time away from the ranch, and being in Delta's company, even though the tension that still hovered between them. He'd been able to relax for a few short moments, and somehow that new beginning he needed finally seemed possible.

"THERE'S MY BOY!" Jake ran across the yard and jumped into Delta's arms. At fifty-five pounds, he was no lightweight, but she didn't care. He licked the side of her face as his body wriggled against hers. "I missed you, too. Did you have fun today?"

Delta's Australian shepherd loved ranch life and her clients enjoyed having him around, but twice a week she treated him to BowWowWowzer's Doggie Daycare where he could be among his own kind. It was her way of giving back to the animal who gave her so much unconditional love and support through the darkest days of her life.

That darkness had come flooding back when Garrett told her about Rebecca. Not that it was ever completely gone, but on most days, she managed to keep those memories neatly tucked away.

"Thanks for taking such good care of him, Anna." Delta pulled a folded check out of her back pocket and handed it to the daycare's owner. "I think I was paid up until today. This should cover the rest of January and all of February. If not, let me know next week."

"No problem. My Sugar and Banjo can't get enough of him. I swear the three of them together rule the play yard." A chilly twilight breeze blew between them, causing Anna to pull her jacket tighter across her chest. "The temperature is expected to drop tonight. Why aren't you wearing a coat?"

Delta glanced down at her flannel-covered arms. "I guess I forgot to put it on. It's in the truck. I have Jake to keep me warm."

"Far be it from me to pry, but are you all right? You look kind of pale."

Delta lifted her gaze to see two sets of blue eyes studying her closely. Jake's and Anna's.

"What? No." Delta hugged Jake closer to her. "I mean yes, I'm fine. I have a lot of work stuff on my mind tonight."

"If you're sure that's all it is. I know Jake's a good listener but I can lend an ear if you ever need one."

"I appreciate that. You better get inside before you freeze. I'll see you soon."

Delta carried Jake to the truck. He was perfectly fine to walk, but she wasn't willing to release her hold on him. She needed the comfort only he could provide. Once tucked away in the warmth of the cab, she eased her grip on him, but he refused to budge from her lap. He sensed her hurt and grief and protectively shielded her from the world just as he'd done from day one.

Anna stood watching her from the daycare's front door. If she didn't leave now, Delta was certain the woman would knock on her window next. She backed out of the drive and started down the road with Jake plastered to her side. Turning on the radio, she tried to forget her conversation with Garrett. It was impossible when guilt wrapped its icy fingers around her heart. Delta was all too familiar with cancer. She had survived stage IIIb Hodgkin's lymphoma after it had almost killed her three years ago. That was when Jake had come into her life.

Her father had heard about a litter of puppies from one of his customers. Cute as Jake was, the last thing she'd wanted was an animal to care for. She'd been back living with her parents and couldn't even take care of herself. But once she looked into the dog's big blue eyes, her heart had melted. From that point forward, they rarely spent time away from one another. He'd gone with her to the hospital, giving comfort and support not just to her, but to other patients. Once she had kicked cancer's ass, she worked with Jake to have him become a certified therapy dog. They visited hospitals and nursing homes in Missoula, and still did, whenever she went home. But they'd also continued their routine here in Saddle Ridge.

Jake wasn't just her dog. He was her best friend and had never let her down.

She pulled down the ranch drive to her small home and parked. She rented the former caretaker's home on an older couple's ranch. They were on one side of the property and Delta on the other. In exchange for the use of their barn to house her farrier equipment and work truck, she shod their horses free of charge.

She opened the truck door, allowing Jake to jump over her lap and onto the ground. Every night he ran to her landlord's door for a cookie, then back to her house for dinner.

Delta slid into her jacket and sat in one of the rockers on the back porch. The brisk January air felt good against her warm skin. Between the nachos and her dinner, she felt a food coma coming on. She leaned her head back, closing her eyes. Garrett's face immediately came to mind. The sadness in his eyes as he spoke of Rebecca had just about broken her. If she hadn't left when she had, she never would have made it out of there tear free. Why had she survived when so many others had died? People with families. People like Rebecca. They'd both battled cancer at the same time, yet she—the one with no family—had survived.

A soggy tennis ball landed in her lap, jarring her out

of her thoughts. "Ew, Jake!" Delta held up the filthy ball. "Is this the one you lost last summer?" Jake ran down the steps and barked, waiting for her to throw it. "I'll take that as a yes. One more time then we're going in." She stood and threw the ball of crud toward the empty pasture before unlocking the back door. Within seconds, Jake had returned with his treasure. "You're not bringing that in the house. Drop it." If she didn't know better, she would have sworn he rolled his eyes at her. "Yeah, I know. Mean mommy. Now come inside for dinner. I have a date with the TV remote."

She wondered what Garrett was doing tonight. She imagined him curled up on a couch, reading to his kids. Did they look like him? Not that it mattered. She couldn't go there. She made a point to avoid any personal involvement with a client. This was still a new business and she wouldn't screw it up. There wasn't room or time for dating.

She sagged against the kitchen counter. She'd never missed the touch of a man more than she did right now. And only one man would do. Garrett Slade. The most off-limits man she knew.

Chapter Three

The following morning, Jake beat Delta into the Silver Bells Ranch stables. Normally she wouldn't have minded, but not knowing how Garrett would react, she quickly caught up to her over-curious dog. She didn't want anything to rekindle yesterday's tension.

Delta turned the corner and saw Garrett crouched down in front of Jake scratching his ears and talking to him. "Where did you come from?"

"I'm sorry. He's with me."

Garrett smiled up at her and then ruffled her pup's long blue merle fur. "Let me guess." Her dog panted happily at the attention. "This is Jake."

"The one and only." Delta patted her thigh, signaling for him to come to her side. "I hope it's okay that he's here. He goes to work with me on most days."

"It's fine. Dylan told me. I wish my daughter was here to see him. She would be in love. I keep thinking about getting a dog to help her adjust to the move." Garrett took off his hat and raked his hand through his thick brown hair before setting it back on his head. "And I'm rambling again."

"Good morning, Delta," Dr. Lydia Presley said as

she and her assistant exited Lightning Bug's stall. "I'm glad you could be here today."

"Hey, Lydia." Delta was thankful for the intrusion. "No problem. I'm anxious to see how he's progressing."

"I just finished taking the x-rays. I got here a little early." She held out a slender, deeply tanned hand to Garrett. "We haven't met yet. I'm Lydia Presley, your veterinarian, and this is my assistant, Selena. I hope you don't mind that we went ahead and got started."

"Not at all. I'm Garrett, new co-owner of the ranch. It's a pleasure to meet you. My brother speaks highly of you."

"Same here. I've heard a lot about you, as well."

Apparently, Lydia had heard more about Garrett than she had. She had known the brothers had partnered but that had been the extent of it. It would have been nice to know something about him before they met, not that anyone owed her that. But the man piqued her curiosity in the worst possible way.

"Garrett, how familiar are you with navicular disease?" Lydia asked.

He shook his head. "I've heard of it, but I've never had to deal with it before."

"Let's begin with the basics, then. It's a degenerative disease of the navicular bone. Don't think of it as a disease the horse contracted. It's more of a syndrome of abnormalities and it's commonly misdiagnosed, which is why x-rays give a more definitive picture." Lydia tugged her iPad out of her bag and flipped open the cover. Tapping on the screen, she opened a series of digital x-rays and pointed to a small bone located on the backside of the front hoof. "It also affects the tendon behind it, and this little sac between the bone and the tendon. It's not something that happens overnight. While many times it's attributed to incorrect shoeing, that wasn't the case here."

"Then what caused it?"

"We don't know for sure. Quarter horses like Lightning Bug are more prone to it. They have large bodies on small feet. It was probably a trauma of some sort that resulted in an interruption of the blood supply. There's no cure, but we can manage it with drug therapy, exercise and the use of a nerve block. We've already discontinued drug therapy due to his improvement. Today we're looking to see what adjustments need to be made to his shoe."

"Which is where I come in," Delta said. "In this case, I used a light plastic and aluminum glue-on shoe with a foam insert, similar to our own running shoes. It's critical the hoof angles and balance are correct so Lightning Bug has the correct foot support. That's why we're checking to see if any adjustments need to be made since the hoof is continually growing."

"And you're sure you can handle all of this?"

Delta ground her back teeth together. She knew he didn't mean anything derogatory with his question, but somehow she doubted he would have asked it if he had been dealing with her father instead.

"I've been handling it," she answered. "I have quite a bit of experience with corrective shoeing and navicular disease."

"And we've successfully managed it together on several horses." There was a slight edge to Lydia's voice. "It's not that uncommon. We treated one of your sister-in-law's rescues before Christmas. I want Lightning Bug to continue with daily light exercise to keep him moving. This is not something you want to baby, because stall rest will do more harm than good. I'll be back to check on him midweek. Since Delta's modifying the shoe, we like to make sure everything is doing what it should."

Delta wasn't upset but she appreciated Lydia's support. If Garrett picked up on the women's tension, he didn't show it. The man had a lot on his shoulders now that he was the ranch's co-owner. It had to be difficult being a single parent and starting over.

Delta checked her watch. It wasn't even nine o'clock and she had already emptied her thermos of coffee. She left Lydia and Garrett to discuss the other horses in the stables and headed toward the new lounge area he'd told her about last night over dinner, praying there was a freshly brewed pot.

Delta yawned, cursing herself for staying awake half the night. It hadn't exactly been her choice. She couldn't get her conversation with Garrett out of her head. Every time she had closed her eyes, there he was. The man was good-looking, she'd give him that. But that didn't mean she wanted him invading her every waking thought.

Jake trotted along next to her as she entered the lounge. She had expected one table and a handful of chairs, not several tables and a mini cafeteria setup. The mismatched furniture gave it a cozy feel. There were even Crock-Pots plugged in along the back wall, most likely courtesy of some of the ranch hands' wives that worked up at the lodge.

"Great." Delta looked down at Jake. "Now he's given

me a reason to like him. I don't want to like him." The dog nudged her hand with his wet nose. "Don't you get too attached to him either."

She'd met many widows and widowers over the last three years. She'd visited with children too young to understand what was happening to their bodies. Those were the hardest. But out of everyone she'd met, Garrett was different. The people she sat with were going through cancer or had gone through it repeatedly. Garrett had suffered through the ordeal long-term, and three years later the loss of his wife still haunted him. Maybe that was why she couldn't get him out of her head.

"Delta, do you have a minute?" A shiver ran up and down her spine at the sound of his voice.

"Sure." Delta reached for a tall paper cup and filled it to the top. "Coffee?"

"Yes, please."

She watched him shift uncomfortably from the corner of her eye. "Tell me when. I always take mine black so I never know how much creamer people use."

Garrett waved his hand. "That's good." Delta handed him the cup. "About before... I don't want you to think I'm questioning your abilities."

"Aren't you?" Delta faced him. "I'll admit, I was a little miffed, but I realize you're concerned about Lightning Bug. I don't know how much Dylan told you about my experience, so I'll fill you in because you should know who's working for you."

"Delta, you don't have to do that." Garrett set his cup on the table behind him.

"Yes, I do. It's the only way you'll begin to trust me."

"If Dylan trusts you then I trust you." He sighed and

jammed both hands in his pockets. "But if it makes you feel better, tell me."

"I'm a Certified Journeyman Farrier by the American Farrier's Association. I have both my forging and therapeutic endorsements. I also make a point to continue my education on a regular basis and I consistently work closely with equine veterinarians and hospitals throughout the state. I'm a fourth-generation farrier and this is more than just a job to me. It's my life. It's been ingrained in me since I could walk. And if there's anything I'm uncertain about, I have an extensive network to confer with."

"Wow, no wonder my brother was afraid I'd run you off." There was a nervous lilt to Garrett's voice. For a man who had greeted her so cocksure yesterday, she rather enjoyed the softer side of him. Maybe too much so. He stiffened as if reading her thoughts. "I appreciate your understanding. And I wanted to thank you for last night. It was nice having a friend to talk to."

There was that word again. She didn't want to be in the friend zone. Friends did things together. Friends relied on one another. The only thing she wanted to rely on Garrett for was a paycheck.

"If you need to talk, I'm available to listen, but—"

"That's what I had started to say before Dr. Presley joined us. I enjoy talking to you. I felt human for the first time in a long time last night. So, yeah, I'd like to take you to dinner sometime soon."

"Garrett." One of the ranch hands poked his head in the door. "We have a grain delivery coming in."

"Okay, be right there."

"Thanks for understanding about earlier." Garrett

slapped a plastic top on his coffee. "I'll call you and we'll make plans."

And then he was gone.

"What the heck just happened?" She slumped in one of the chairs and began scratching Jake's scruff. "Did he just ask me out on a date?" Jake lifted his paw and rested it on her thigh. Delta groaned and closed her eyes. This was not how she planned to start the morning.

BY THE TIME Kacey stepped off the school bus, Garrett was ready to call it a day. He still had a few hours of work to do, but it would have to wait until tomorrow morning. He wanted to spend a few hours with Kacey before they went to his brother Harlan's house for dinner. Over Christmas, he had promised Kacey and his seven-year-old niece Ivy that once they moved to town they could have regular weekend sleepovers. This was supposed to be his turn to host, but the girls were staying at Harlan's since Garrett wasn't finished unpacking. That was next on his agenda.

Emma had offered to babysit Bryce on Saturday while Dylan helped him finish setting up the house. By the time Kacey got home on Sunday night, he wanted their place looking like a real home. They hadn't had a home of their own since Rebecca died. He loved living close to family again. They could support him when he needed it. He'd missed that in Wyoming. Rebecca's family was wonderful, but it wasn't the same as having his own nearby.

Instead of embarrassing Kacey again on the snowmobile, he opted to pick her up in the SUV. Surely that had to be okay. In spring, he'd allow her to walk from the ranch's front gate to the house, but it was just too cold in mid-January.

Kacey slammed the passenger door and glanced in the backseat at Bryce. "Are we going to Uncle Harlan's now?"

"Not until later." Garrett stared at his daughter. "You could try saying hello first." Once again he was met with radio silence. "Kacey, look at me." When she refused, he cut the truck's ignition.

"What are you doing?" she screeched and looked toward the school bus pulling away from the ranch. "Just drive."

"Listen, young lady. I realize you're having a difficult time accepting this move. But this is home now. I suggest you find a few things you like about it and focus on those because we're not moving back to Wyoming. And from now on, when you get in this car you say hello to me and your brother. And you need to stop yelling and slamming things. Do I make myself clear?"

"Yes," she murmured, still facing the window.

"Can you look at me, please?"

Kacey turned her body slightly toward him, and stared at the floor.

"Looking at me involves me seeing your eyes."

Slowly she lifted her gaze to his. Tearstains streaked her cheeks and her eyes were pink-tinged and puffy.

"Have you been crying?"

She blinked once as her bottom lip began to quiver. "I'm just tired, Daddy."

Garrett wasn't buying that excuse. "If you're too tired, then maybe we shouldn't go to Uncle Harlan's tonight."

Kacey's eyes grew wild. "You said every weekend Ivy and I could have sleepovers. You can't break your promise."

"Well, honey, if you're so tired that you were crying on the way home from school—"

"I just need a nap."

His daughter had never once asked for a nap. When she was little, she always fought her mother when she tried to get her to take one. Something was wrong and he wanted to know who or what had upset his daughter.

"I wish you would talk to me and tell me what's bothering you."

"Can we go home now?"

Garrett wanted communication with his kid that went beyond one-line answers. A few weeks ago, this hadn't been a problem. Now it had become their normal routine and he hated it.

"Yeah, we can go." Garrett started the truck. "Do you have homework this weekend?"

"A little."

"How about you start on it before we go to your uncle's house." At least that would keep her in the kitchen where he could help her.

"Ivy and I were going to do it together."

"Together better mean you do your homework and she does hers. Not you do one subject and she does another, then you copy off each other like you did last week." That was a problem with having cousins in the same grade.

"We won't copy." Kacey already had her fingers wrapped around the door handle as they pulled up in front of the house. No sooner did he park than she was out of the truck and up the stairs and jiggling the knob. She would just have to wait a minute because the door was locked and he still needed to get Bryce out of his car seat. "Daddy, I have to go to the bathroom. Can I have the keys?"

Garrett sighed, not knowing whether to believe her or not. She did have an hour-long bus ride home. Deciding he'd had enough battles with his daughter for one day, he tossed her the keys. "Leave them on the kitchen table, please."

By the time he got inside with Bryce, she had firmly shut herself behind her bedroom door. Just as he figured. He wanted to knock. Hell, he wanted to drag her out of her room and hug her until she opened up to him, but he knew she'd have no part of it. He missed his sweet little girl.

She used to be the perpetually happy kid. He always knew where she was by her laughter. That all changed when Rebecca died. The anniversary was eleven days before Kacey's birthday, and his in-laws always made such a production of the date, it clouded Kacey's special day. This year he had decided his daughter deserved to have a happy birthday. Maybe then he'd hear her laugh again.

THREE HOURS LATER, Garrett helped his brother clear the table while his sister-in-law tried to teach Bryce how to eat and not wear his dinner.

"Good luck with that, Belle." He laughed. "I used to think it was a hand-eye coordination issue, because he appears to miss his mouth, but he's been tested for everything under the sun. One doctor told me he thinks

Bryce likes the feel of the food, that's why he wears it. It's also the reason we never eat at a restaurant."

Belle held a forkful of food out to Bryce. "If you can eat this nicely, then you'll get another." Bryce frowned and reached for the plate, but Belle pulled it away. "One mouthful at a time, sweetheart. Finish this first."

"Daddy, can we go play in my room?" Ivy asked. Kacey hadn't said two words to him since their talk earlier, but she'd chatted nonstop with her cousin since they walked in the door.

"Go ahead, but be back in a half hour for dessert."

"No copying each other's homework," Garrett reminded them.

"You seriously don't think they went upstairs to do homework, do you?" Harlan asked.

Garrett waited until he no longer heard the girls' footsteps on the stairs before answering. "Has Ivy mentioned anything about Kacey being upset in school or on the bus?"

"Not to me." Belle wiped Bryce's face with a napkin and handed him a spoonful of baked beans. "Did something happen?"

"When she came home today, she had obviously been crying. I tried to talk to her about it, but I couldn't get anywhere. I just thought maybe she had said something to Ivy."

"No, but I'll see what I can find out," Harlan said.

"Just don't let on that I put you up to it." The last thing Garrett wanted was his daughter thinking he was spying on her. He was, and owned that, but she didn't need to know about it.

"Please." His younger brother nodded to the sheriff's

hat hanging by the back door. "I have my ways of getting people to talk without them knowing it."

"Yeah, that's why you were so successful getting Ivy to confess to taking the neighbor's bunny last year." Belle shook her head. "Kids are complicated. I was one of the worst."

"You sure were," the men said in unison.

"Now, that's not right." Belle wadded up her napkin and threw it at them. "Let me tell you, growing up around you two was no picnic. Now hand me a dish towel. I think I'm getting somewhere with this one."

Garrett admired Harlan and Belle. They had grown up together, gone their separate ways and then found their way back to each other last year. Now they were expecting a baby in May. Despite their playful digs at one another, they were the happiest couple he knew, outside of Dylan and Emma. Garrett had been the first of the five Slade brothers to get married, and he'd never been more sure of something in his entire life. And he'd thought it would last at least fifty years, if not seventy-five, considering they married straight out of high school. He missed that companionship. He missed those knowing glances across the table. Having someone to hold all night long. He missed his old life, and if Kacey felt a fraction of the way he did, he understood where she was coming from.

"In all seriousness," Harlan began, pulling him out of his thoughts. "I'll see what I can find out and let you know. How's it going at Silver Bells this week?"

"Better. I think I'm finally getting to know everyone's names and what they do. I need to get creative on where we can save on the renovations. I think the biggest savings will be in sweat equity and bartering. Maybe a week or weekend at the ranch in exchange for services rendered."

"That's a great idea. I did quite a bit of that when I built the rescue center." Belle's Forever Ranch opened last year on the other side of their property. The non-profit rescued animals and provided desperately needed medical care. Once they were rehabilitated, they helped give comfort to abused and neglected children who had suffered similar fates. "I can give you some of my construction contacts. Maybe they can help you, too."

"I'd appreciate that, thank you." Garrett poured a cup of coffee and sat across from Belle at the table. She had the patience of a saint and didn't coddle Bryce the way his mother-in-law had. Dawn had blamed his messy eating on Rebecca's death, and she'd taken to spoon-feeding him at every meal over the past three years. Garrett had repeatedly asked her not to, but she insisted on feeding him the way Rebecca had. His son had been sixteen months when Rebecca passed. It didn't matter that he'd grown old enough to eat by himself.

"Dylan told me you and Delta had dinner together last night." Harlan grabbed another dish towel from the drawer and set it on the table for Belle. "I really like her. I'm glad you're getting out."

"You're seeing Delta?" Belle's face lit up brighter than the sun on the horizon. "Just in time for Valentine's Day. She is so nice. I can't even begin to tell you how much she's done for my rescues."

"Whoa!" Garrett pushed away from the table, almost taking his coffee with him. "I am not seeing Delta. I made that clear to Dylan last night. Let's not perpetuate that rumor."

"Calm down, bro." Harlan wiped up the coffee that sloshed onto the table. "No need to get all defensive. I'm just telling you what Dylan told me. But if you enjoy being around one another, why not see where it goes."

"Because I'm married." Garrett hated that people automatically assumed that because his wife died the marriage was over. Maybe it was in the eyes of the law, but it wasn't for him. He'd always hated the phrase "'til death do us part." He didn't believe in it and had asked the minister to remove it from their wedding vows fifteen years ago. They vowed to love each other for all eternity instead, and he would never break that promise, even though she had told him she hoped he would find someone new one day. There wasn't room in his heart to love another woman. "We're just friends."

"Okay, fine." Harlan shrugged at Belle. "Just make sure she knows that."

"Of course she does." Garrett shook his head. "I didn't even know she would be at the Iron Horse when I went there. I saw her at the bar, and we ate a meal together. It's not like I asked her out." Garrett froze, remembering his earlier conversation with Delta. "Oh, no."

"What's wrong?" Belle asked.

"I think I accidentally asked Delta out to dinner."

Harlan slapped his brother on the back and laughed. "The heart wants what the heart wants."

Garrett closed his eyes. This couldn't be happening. How could he have been so cavalier with his dinner invite? Maybe she hadn't taken it that way. He replayed the conversation in his mind. What exactly had he said? Something along the lines of wanting to take her to dinner. *Shit!* He had asked her out and hadn't even realized it. He scrubbed his hands down his face. He needed to straighten that out and fast.

Chapter Four

"Why do I get the feeling you're avoiding me?" Garrett startled her as she exited Lightning Bug's stall.

"Good Lord." Delta flattened herself against the wall before realizing who it was. "You would have been in for the surprise of your life if I'd been carrying a hot shoe."

"I knew you weren't since your truck is outside and the back was shut." He crossed his arms in front of his chest. "No forger, no hot shoes. I also saw Jake waiting patiently behind the wheel for you."

Okay, so he was observant. "I've been here almost every day to check on Lightning Bug, except for Sunday when I visited my family. I was only stopping in for a minute."

"I know you've been here." He widened his stance and tilted his hat back. "I got your notes, Delta. It's just I haven't seen you in a week."

Five days, but who was counting. But he was right. She had been avoiding him. Luckily for her Garrett was a creature of habit and it didn't take long to figure out his routine. She'd been able to get in and out without running into him, except for today, when he beat her at her own game.

"Listen I think we should—"

"I have to tell you—" they both said at the same time.

"Ladies first." Garrett removed his hat and bowed slightly before her. The gesture, however goofy, was actually charming in a Garrett Slade sort of way.

"Look, I—I like you," she began, trying to find the words to let him down easy.

"Okay." Garrett quickly donned his hat. "Let me stop you there. I gave you the wrong impression the other day. I think you're very nice but I don't want to date you."

Delta started to laugh. "Oh, thank God for small favors."

"Excuse me?" Garrett stepped back and frowned slightly. She hadn't meant to wound his ego, but those were the best words she'd heard all week.

"I don't want to date you either." Delta patted her chest in relief. "I've been wracking my brains trying to find a way to tell you. I mean you're good-looking and all that, but I refuse to date anyone I work with or for."

Garrett began to smile, seemingly satisfied with her explanation. "I still would like to take you to dinner, though. But it would be strictly platonic. Just friends. Nothing more."

"Yeah, about that." Delta gnawed on her bottom lip. "Don't get offended, but I kind of make a point not to hang with anyone I work with either. If the friendship goes south, it affects my business. If you don't mind, I'd like to keep that part of my life separate. Unless you need someone impartial to talk to about your wife or something like that."

"Okay, now I'm confused." Garrett stared at her as if she had three heads. "It's okay for me to talk to you about something painfully personal but we're not allowed to be friends? I think your logic is a little backwards."

"No, it's not." Delta sighed. She hadn't meant to hurt his feelings. "Listening to someone talk is different. It's what I do, well, we do. Jake's a certified therapy dog and I volunteer at the convalescent home in town. I understand the need to talk. Your loss was devastating and I'm always available if you just need someone to hear you out. That's a given. But it can't be more than that."

"How do you make friends, then?" Garrett's face contorted.

"I have friends." Delta didn't like having to defend her reasons for not mixing work and pleasure. "Here and back home."

"Back home, huh?" He rested an arm on a stack of hay bales. "You sound like my daughter."

"I don't understand." And she didn't care to. This was exactly why she kept her personal life private.

"You live in Saddle Ridge. You've been here for— what did you say—a year?"

Delta nodded and played along. "What does that have to do with anything?"

"You've established a business and a reputation here. Quite a good one from what I understand. Whether you want to admit it or not, this is your home. Missoula is where you're from."

Delta opened her mouth to argue and quickly shut

it. Okay, so he had a slight point. But, Missoula would always be home, no matter where she lived or for however long. "How about we agree to disagree and leave it at that."

He studied her for a few seconds before answering. "Sure." She began to walk away when he continued, "One of the Belgians threw a shoe. Do you think you might be able to fit that in today?"

Delta inwardly groaned. There were a lot of things she loved about her job but shoeing an uncooperative draft horse wasn't one of them. It would have been nice if he had at least considered her comments about the ranch not having a shoeing stall. She realized he was trying to save money, but a shoeing stall worked to Dr. Presley's advantage, too. It gave them both much more control over the animal while keeping stress to a minimum.

She checked her watch. "Yeah, I can squeeze it in. I'll have to open up the doors and back my truck in."

"Thank you. Let me know if you need anything."

Delta watched him walk away. She was okay with her decision to not be friends. Wasn't she? He was a customer. Her largest. Going out and having a few drinks or dinner would be unprofessional. People in town would talk and assume they were dating. Or that Silver Bells was getting a special rate. Well…they *were* getting special treatment. Garrett did just want to be friends. Nothing more. And he was still in love with Rebecca. Maybe it wouldn't be so bad. Then again, she already found herself drawn to the man, and she didn't need any more temptation. It would only lead to heartbreak. Hers.

AN HOUR LATER, Garrett cursed himself for allowing Delta to get under his skin. Not because she'd done something wrong, but because he couldn't get her scent out of his nose. It was a combination of cinnamon and nutmeg, and he couldn't figure out if it was her hair, or some sort of body wash she had used. Either way, he'd never smelled that scent on another person before. It was uniquely Delta and it drove him crazy.

Fresh air. Now, that was what the doctor ordered. The day had been unseasonably warm, to the point where excessive runoff from the snow melt had begun to flood one of their stables. Luckily it was the side where they stored some of their equipment, so none of the horses were standing in water. They'd had to rush-order a load of sandbags to prevent any further flooding. It was one more expense they didn't need.

Garrett rechecked the grounds surrounding all three stables and then fired up one of their four-wheelers to tour the ranch's perimeter. Normally his ranch hands made the trek around the 730 acres, but he wanted to distance himself from all things Delta. He saw her truck drive toward the main gate as he crested the first slush-covered hill. The last thing he needed was to start changing his routine to distract himself from a woman. There was no other woman. Only Rebecca. Then why did he feel so damn guilty?

Garrett's sanity began to return by the time he finished riding fence. He checked the time—something he did constantly since they'd moved to Saddle Ridge. When he'd lived with his in-laws, he hadn't paid attention to his children's routines. They were just there when he finished working for the day.

It pained him to realize how unaware he'd been until he was a hundred percent responsible for them. He had always considered himself a great parent, when in reality, he hadn't been. He'd blamed Dawn and Terry for many of the kids' problems but he'd waited to rectify the situation, and that had also affected his kids. If they'd moved sooner, even to a home of their own in Wheatland, it would've been better than doing nothing.

On his way back to the stables, the shrill ring of his cell phone interrupted his thoughts. He tugged the phone from his breast pocket and checked the display. It was Kacey's school.

"Garrett Slade speaking."

"Mr. Slade, this is Darcy Malone from Saddle Ridge Elementary. We just wanted to check on Kacey since she wasn't in class this morning."

"What do you mean, she's not in class? I watched her get on the school bus this morning."

"Kacey's homeroom teacher reported her absent." Garrett heard the muffled sound of somebody covering the phone. "Mr. Slade, I'm going to personally check each of her classes and call you back in a few minutes."

"What? You expect me just to wait when you have no idea where my daughter is? I'm on my way there."

Garrett jammed his phone in his pocket and pinned the throttle as far as it would go. His tires spun before they gripped the ground. He skidded the four-wheeler to a stop beside his truck and hopped off, fishing in his pocket for the keys before realizing they were already in the ignition.

He dialed Harlan first. "The school just called me.

They said they haven't seen Kacey today but I saw her get on the bus."

"Where are you now?" Garrett heard Harlan's police siren through the phone.

"Heading to the school."

"I'll call it in and meet you there. Try to stay calm. She's probably somewhere in the building. I'll have them pull Ivy out of class and see if she knows anything."

Garrett threw his phone on the passenger seat. He knew something was off with his daughter. He had tried to be her friend, hoping she would talk to him. Maybe he should've just demanded she tell him what was going on. Even after her mother's death, Kacey hadn't been this withdrawn. Dylan had been right. There was no way he could've comprehended the difficulties of switching schools and making friends when he'd never had to do it. Had he pushed her too far?

His phone rang again. "Mr. Slade, it's Darcy. Kacey is not in school."

Garrett's heart stopped beating as the world went silent around him. He tried to breathe as the phone slipped from his fingers, but his lungs no longer functioned. He pulled his truck off the road, unable to feel the steering wheel beneath his palms.

"Mr. Slade? Mr. Slade…"

Garrett fought for air.

"Mr. Slade. Are you still there?"

"Where's my daughter?" he whispered. "I can't lose her, too."

"I think I can hear him. I don't know if he got into an

accident or what. Mr. Slade, if you're still there, we've notified the sheriff's department."

"Harlan." Garrett shook his head and sucked in a deep breath of air. "My brother's the sheriff's department," he said as he patted the driver's side floorboard for the phone.

"Mr. Slade, I can barely hear you."

His fingertips grazed the hard plastic of the phone. He inched it toward him until he could grip it. He pressed the Bluetooth button and waited for the familiar chime. "I'm here. My brother Harlan is the deputy sheriff. He's already on the way. I'll be there in two minutes."

Garrett pulled onto the road as Harlan's police SUV flew up behind him. He lowered the window and signaled for his brother to pass. *Harlan will find her.* He had to. *This is fixable.* It had to be. *This isn't like when Rebecca died.* It can't be.

An hour after she had left, Delta returned to Silver Bells in search of her phone. The stables seemed eerily quiet as she walked through the door with Jake by her side. Come to think of it, she hadn't seen a single soul when she drove onto the ranch, which was odd for that time of day.

"I wonder where everyone is." Delta's boots against the cement corridor and an occasional neigh were the only sounds to be heard. "Maybe they were having a company meeting up at the guest lodge. You need to help mommy find her phone."

She scanned the center corridor as Jake trotted ahead of her. Stopping at Lightning Bug's stall, she started to unlatch the door when she heard the faint sound of music coming from the next stall down. The stall that had been empty since she started working on the ranch.

"Hello?" Delta called out. She peered through the upper bars of the stall wall, not seeing anyone, but the music was definitely louder. It almost sounded as if it was coming from under her. She tried to look down along the wall, but the stall was partially swathed in a dark shadow. "Hello?" The stall door creaked as she opened it and the music grew louder. "Is someone in here?"

She allowed her eyes to adjust to the dim light before slowly peering around the corner. She made out the faint outline of a child's shoe.

Oh, my God. There's a kid on the floor.

Delta rushed into the stall and reached into the darkness. A scream pierced the air and sent her to her knees. Jake rushed in, barking incessantly in the dark. A tiny figure scampered past her and into the corridor as Delta regained her footing. She gripped the stall's bars, pulling herself to her feet only to be standing in front of a very much alive little girl who was equally as startled as she was. It didn't help that Jake was continually circling her.

"Come here, Jake. She doesn't need to be herded. She's okay." Delta bent forward. "You are okay, aren't you?"

Delta heard the music again, and realized it was coming from the girl's earbuds. She'd had her iPod on so loud she hadn't heard Delta coming. The girl nodded, but her frightened face said otherwise. Her eyes wildly looked up and down the corridor but not at her and Jake.

She didn't seem afraid of them. But she was afraid of something.

"My name is Delta, and this is Jake. Jake, say hello." The dog sat in front of the girl and waved his right paw at her. "Jake's a therapy dog, so if you're scared, you can hold on to him and he'll make you feel better. Do you want to touch him?"

Delta wanted to get close enough to the child to make sure there weren't any visible signs of trauma. The girl lifted her hand so Jake could sniff her. He pushed his head under her fingers until they were buried in his long thick coat. The corners of her mouth began to lift as Jake pressed his body against hers.

"What's your name?" Delta asked.

"Kacey," she whispered.

Kacey? Garrett's Kacey? "Don't you have school today?"

She shook her head. "We have off."

Hmm. Delta could have sworn she passed the school bus in town earlier. "How would you like to help me find my phone. I think I dropped it here earlier when I was checking on Lightning Bug."

"Are you a vet?"

"No, sweetie. I'm a farrier. I put shoes on horses."

"How come you had to check on Lightning Bug?"

"Because he has a limp and needed a different type of shoe, so I had to make him one. You could say I'm a shoe designer for horses."

Kacey's smile began to grow. "I know where your phone is."

"You do? Where?"

She disappeared into the stall and returned carrying a yellow *Beauty and the Beast* backpack. So much for her not having school today. She unzipped the front pocket and removed Delta's phone. "I found it when I came in before. I was going to give it to my dad later."

"Thank you for taking care of it for me." Delta punched in her security code and saw a missed call from Garrett. She also noticed the time on the top of the screen. It wasn't even one-thirty and school didn't get out for another hour. "Sweetie, did you walk home from school?"

Kacey shrugged her shoulders and then sat on the floor next to Jake.

"School's a long way from here." It had to be at least three miles. That was a long walk for a child, especially in the cold. Delta pressed the voice mail screen and read the transcribed message. Even without hearing Garrett's voice, the tone was frantic.

She typed a quick text message to him: Found Kacey in your stables. She is okay. I'll stay with her until you arrive.

She pressed Send and slid the phone in the pocket of her jeans.

"How about a snack and a cup of hot chocolate?"

Kacey's eyes brightened at the mention of food. Considering how long it had to have taken her to walk to the ranch, she probably hadn't eaten since breakfast.

"Come on, Jake. Let's get Kacey something to eat."

They both followed her into the new employee lounge. Delta opened the upper cabinets and pulled out a small pack of cookies and a granola bar. She set them on the table, hoping Kacey wouldn't try to run. Although, the way Jake kept body checking her, she didn't think the kid would get very far if she did. That was the one problem with owning an Australian shepherd. They always had to be working, and sometimes that meant herding people.

Delta tore a packet of hot chocolate open and dumped it in a cup before filling it with water. She popped it in the microwave and waited. Kacey unzipped her ski jacket. That was a sign she was staying. Delta stirred the cocoa when the microwave dinged and topped it with a dash of vanilla creamer to cool it down a bit.

"Here you go." Delta set the cup on the table.

Kacey had already slipped out of her coat and was seated. When she reached for the cup, Delta saw tiny bruises on the girl's forearm. They looked like grip marks, about the size of a child's hand. Delta knew them well.

"Kacey, is someone bullying you at school?"

The little girl's eyes flew open. Her panic had returned. Jake instantly sensed her anxiety and began nudging her hand. She reached into his thick fur again and gripped it.

"It's okay to tell me. You should always tell a grown-up when other kids pick on you." Delta sat across from Kacey at the table and watched her expression, seeing parts of Garrett in her tiny features. The same dark hair and eyes. "When I was your age, there was a girl who used to pick on me something terrible. She'd wait until we went into the bathroom and would always push me against the wall and hit me. She did it every day for two years before a teacher caught her. I used to go home and cry. I couldn't understand why she didn't like me."

Kacey's hands stilled. "Really?"

"Really. When the teacher walked in on her doing it, I was so relieved. But you know what I found out? I could have told my teacher or my parents and they would have put a stop to it much sooner."

"Weren't you afraid?" Kacey began to bite her thumbnail.

"Yes, I was. I thought if I told, then other kids would start picking on me. But that didn't happen. The teacher made sure of it. They moved that girl into another class." Delta wondered what the policy was at Kacey's school. Maybe the kid would even be expelled. The bruises on her arm were pretty dark. Whoever did this to her used force. "Have you tried talking to your daddy?"

Kacey shook her head. That would explain why she was hiding out. She didn't want to get in trouble for skipping school.

"Kacey!" Delta heard Garrett's voice boom through the stables.

Kacey wrapped her arms around Jake. "He's going to be so mad at me."

"He's not mad, he's scared." Delta stood. "Stay here with Jake and I'll explain it to him first, okay?" She scanned the room to make sure there wasn't a back door she might have overlooked earlier. Nope, just one door. She stepped into the corridor, almost slamming into Garrett. "Slow down, cowboy. We need to talk first."

Garrett tried to step around her, but she blocked him again. Flattening her hands on his chest, she pushed him out of the doorway. Delta saw fear reflecting in his eyes.

"She's okay, but you need to listen to me for one second before you go in there, please." Delta refused to let him in, afraid he'd yell at her for cutting class.

"Someone has been bullying your daughter and from the bruises I just saw on her arm, I think it's been pretty bad. I'm assuming she headed home shortly after the bus dropped her off at school."

"What?" Garrett's body stiffened. "Somebody hurt my baby?"

"What's going on?" Harlan joined them, out of breath. "Where's Kacey?"

"I want to know who hurt my kid." Garrett stared down at Delta, willing her to move.

"I think the bruises are from another child's grip," she said as she moved aside and let him pass.

Garrett crossed the room in three long strides and lifted his daughter into his arms, sobbing into her hair. "You scared me, baby. Don't you ever do that again. I can't lose you."

Delta turned away to give him privacy and faced Harlan. "She didn't say much, but she was very interested when I told her I had been bullied as a kid. I'll leave the rest to you guys."

"Thank you, Delta." Harlan tipped his hat and entered the lounge.

She patted her thigh and Jake trotted out of the room to her. "Come on, boy. You did good today. You deserve an extra cookie tonight."

Her heart broke for Garrett. Their family had suffered enough and now they were struggling once again. They may have moved from Wyoming for a fresh start, but that didn't always come easy. Maybe Garrett needed a friend more than she needed her rules.

Chapter Five

"I know you're scared, sweetheart, but you can tell me anything. No matter what it is." Hours later, Garrett still fought to remain calm. He was finding it increasingly difficult when he still didn't know who'd hurt his daughter. And until he found out, she wasn't going back to school. "If you don't want to talk to me, you can always talk to your uncle Dylan or Emma or your uncle Harlan and aunt Belle."

"What about Delta?" Kacey shifted on the couch and looked up at him.

"When someone hurts you, I want you to tell any adult." He hadn't expected Kacey to include Delta in her circle of trust. Then again, Delta had been the one to get her to finally open up. "Did you like talking to her?"

Kacey nodded. "She told me someone had bullied her, too."

The revelation surprised him along with the anger coursing through his veins at the thought of somebody hurting Delta. He had no right to feel anything for her except gratitude. He wanted to tell his daughter she could talk to Delta whenever she wanted. While he didn't think Delta would be opposed to it, their conversation earlier about not being friends reverberated in his head. His heart told him she'd make an exception for a child.

There was a knock at his front door before Harlan entered. "I wanted to check on you two before I headed home." Harlan joined them on the couch. "How are you doing, buttercup?"

His brother looked over her head and nodded toward the door.

"Kacey, why don't you go get ready for bed. I'll be in to read you a story in a little bit."

Wordlessly, she slipped off the couch and trudged up the stairs to her room.

"Good night, Kacey," his brother called after her.

"Good night, Uncle Harlan."

As soon as her bedroom door clicked shut, Harlan turned to him. "Belle and I were able to get more out of Ivy tonight. It's not just one kid bullying her, it's a group. A little mean girls club. And they've not only attacked her physically, they've been saying things about her online. Ivy couldn't tell me what, because we don't allow her to have any social media accounts. She had only heard about it from her friends. I went on there pretending to be one of her classmates and I saw some pretty hateful things."

"What the hell is wrong with kids today?" Garrett slammed his fist into the couch. "We didn't do this when we were their age."

"We didn't have social media back then, but there was bullying." Harlan got up and walked into the kitchen. "I remember quite a few kids getting beat up on the playground and not saying anything. Delta told me earlier that she had been on the receiving end as a kid."

"Kacey just told me that, too." Garret was beyond thankful Delta had revealed what had to have been a painful past to his daughter. "I think it's the only reason Kacey's talking tonight. She finally realizes she's not alone. How long has Ivy known about this?"

"From what we can gather, from the beginning." Harlan grabbed two beers from the fridge and handed one to Garrett. "They had made a pact not to tell anyone. She didn't want to betray Kacey's trust so she kept it secret and had been trying to defend her. I explained that not saying anything was part of the problem and she promises to tell me or another adult whenever she sees bullying of any kind from now on. I wish I'd had this conversation with her sooner, but at seven years old I didn't think I had to. And I of all people knew better. I hear about this stuff all the time on the job. Children committing suicide because they're being viciously attacked at school. I saw my daughter's name in some of those posts tonight and it sickened me."

Garrett held his head in his hands. *Suicide?* They were talking about little kids. How did he miss the signs? How did he miss the bruises?

"It's hard. She is this little woman so I respect her privacy and let her pick her own outfits and bathe on her own. I never once thought to say show me your arms and legs so I can see if somebody has beaten you up."

"You couldn't have known."

"I should have known." Garrett slammed his beer on the table. "The signs were there. I'm a single father and I took away her only female role model by moving here. I can't help but wonder if she'd have told her grandmother, or if her grandmother would've noticed it earlier and could've put a stop to this."

Harlan patted his brother on the back. "In my experience on the force, kids are pretty good at hiding things. I've seen all sorts of abuse that teachers and neighbors or other parents and siblings had missed. I know you're upset, but don't drive yourself crazy over this. Kacey has other female role models. She's just not used to them yet. She only met Belle and Emma over Christmas. And there's Delta. Kacey clearly trusts her. Maybe they could spend more time together."

"How is that supposed to happen?" Garrett couldn't even get her to agree to dinner. "It would be different if Delta had a kid, too. Then there would be a reason for Kacey to see her. But Delta is long gone before Kacey gets home from school." School. Garrett groaned. "What am I supposed to do now? I can't send her back there. What do I do about these other kids and the stuff online? Whatever's on there, I want it down."

"I've already taken care of her attackers. I reported them to the school board and there is a formal police report on file. I need a statement from you, which is the other reason I'm here. I'll also need a victim statement from Kacey, but that can wait until tomorrow."

"My daughter will be eight in a few weeks and she's already a victim giving statements to the police. When I moved back here, I thought I was moving my kids into a safe environment."

"You have to be vigilant," Harlan said.

"Oh, believe me. Nothing is getting past me again." Garrett wanted to wring the necks of his daughter's tormentors' parents. There was no way kids came by this on their own. They learned it somewhere.

"Maybe Kacey needs to spend more time with Belle at the Forever Ranch. Belle swears by animal assisted therapy."

"So does Delta. Jake is a certified therapy dog."

"I've heard that. Delta has made quite an impression on Saddle Ridge in the year she's been here. She volunteers a lot of her time to various organizations."

"And once again, you're trying to sell me on her."

"Would it be such a bad thing? Dating again doesn't mean you have to stop loving Rebecca. Your heart has more room than you think. Valentine's Day is less than a month away and I'd like to see you happy again. I'm not telling you to marry her. I'm saying explore the possibility of a relationship, whether it be friends or more."

"Please tell me Belle hasn't turned you into one of those people. Valentine's Day is nothing but a greeting card holiday. Even Rebecca didn't buy into it. She felt our love deserved to be celebrated year-round. And you're wrong. There's no room left in my heart."

And there never will be.

A LITTLE MORE than a week had passed since Delta had found Kacey hiding in the stables. She had wanted to call Garrett a few times and ask how she was doing, but she'd decided against it. The kid had a huge support system and she was sure they were taking good care of her.

And it just so happened her next stop was part of that support system. Every six weeks she trimmed hooves at Belle's Forever Ranch along with Harlan's personal stable of horses. She was sure Belle would update her on Kacey.

Delta parked and hopped out of the truck. Jake was at doggie daycare chillin' with his buddies for the day. She missed him when he wasn't with her, but sometimes he just needed to be a dog and not a best friend.

Delta fastened her apron chaps around her waist and gathered her tools before heading to the backside of the stables. "Good morning, darling." Delta rubbed The Fuzz's muzzle. Harlan had named his horses after outlaws and Belle had countered with police ones. She had The Fuzz and Colombo, two rescued former race horses, and Joe Friday, a donkey that had doubled his weight since living at the rescue center.

"Hey, Delta," Belle called to her from the chicken play yard. And it was a real play yard, complete with toys and a little obstacle course. She had never seen a chicken play before she met Belle. "I'll be there in a second. I just need to make sure this one heater is still working on the chicken coop."

"The new coop is adorable." Delta loved Belle's attention to detail. She had built the birds an exact replica of the ranch's red barn, right down to the trim and metal roof.

"It came out good, didn't it?" Belle admired her own handiwork. "I didn't think I'd ever get it finished considering I have to pee every two minutes. I'm with Emma—this pregnancy thing is for the birds." She laughed at her own joke. "Oh, crap." She sighed. "I have to pee again. I'll be right back."

Delta forced a smile as her chest began to tighten. She was happy for Belle, just as she was happy for her friend Liv. But that happiness didn't fill the increasing void in her life. She had dreamt of having children for as long as she could remember. Being one of three kids, she thought she'd at least have that many, but chemotherapy had robbed her of that chance.

Delta inhaled sharply as tears filled her eyes. It had been years since the doctor had confirmed her sterility and the pain never eased, especially since she wasn't eligible to adopt until she was cancer free for five years. Even a private adoption, which she couldn't afford, would be doubtful. It was one more way the big C had kicked her in the teeth. She had a little over two years to go before she could apply and she had the actual date programmed into her phone's calendar.

Some days were more agonizing than others. Today was heading in that direction. Delta wiped at her eyes and turned her attention to The Fuzz.

"Are you ready for me, handsome?" Delta snapped a lead rope to his halter and led him out of the stall. As they walked, she listened to the sound of his bare hooves against the ground. This allowed her to hear any abnormalities in his gait. The fifteen-year-old quarter horse had been shod all his life, but no longer tolerated any form of shoe after his hooves had been so severely neglected they had grown in the shape of a corkscrew. Delta had worked closely with the equine hospital in nearby Kalispell, both donating their services to save the poor animal. Since he spent the majority of his time grazing, they opted to keep his hooves natural to prevent further stress. She stopped by every couple of weeks just to see him and check on his progress. Four months later, he had improved greatly, but still had a long road ahead of him.

She tied him to a nearby hitching post and ran her hand down the front of his leg until she reached his fetlock. She lightly pinched the chestnut on the back of his leg causing him to lift his foot.

"Good boy." She praised him. A race horse would have been trained to lift their foot on command, and at one time, The Fuzz probably had. But he wouldn't do it anymore without a little coaxing on her part. "Let's see what we have going on here." She reached for her hook knife and began cleaning his hoof. "You're doing wonderfully, my dear."

"I'm back." Belle scratched The Fuzz's neck as Delta continued to work. "Have you spoken with Garrett at all?"

That didn't take long to bring him up. "Not since the incident with Kacey. How is she doing?"

"Hard to tell. The kids who bullied her were expelled, but because of what happened, Garrett enrolled her in a private school. It's a lot smaller and she gets more one-on-one instruction, which she desperately needs to bring her grades back up. It didn't help that one of the bullies' parents tried to enroll her daughter in the same place as Kacey."

"They didn't get in, did they?" Kacey deserved a safe learning environment. A kid couldn't concentrate when they constantly had to look over their shoulder. She knew that firsthand.

"No, the school denied the application. They also offer counseling services, but so far, Kacey refuses to participate. We all thought a new school would be a nice do-over for her, but she's starting fresh again." Belle bit her lip. "At least in public school she had Ivy. She was her lifeline. Harlan wants to transfer Ivy to the same school since the kids were cyberbullying her, too. She seems open to it. He and Ivy's mom are planning to sit down this weekend and discuss it further."

"I can't even imagine that whole aspect of it." Delta had thick skin, but she didn't know if she would have been tough enough to handle cyberbullying as a kid. "It's bad enough in school, but when it follows you everywhere you go... Wow."

"I do know that Garrett is grateful to you."

Delta stilled the knife in her hand. "Me? Why?"

"If you hadn't figured it out, who knows how long this would have gone on. Besides, Kacey has asked about you, and she's smitten with Jake."

That thought made Delta smile. "He has that effect on people."

"Kacey is spending the weekend here." Belle walked around the front of the horse until she was standing in front of Delta. "You're more than welcome to stop by. Our door is always open."

"I'm working most of the weekend, but I might be able to squeeze it in."

"Bryce is also staying with us this weekend, in case you wanted to stop by Silver Bells and see Garrett." Delta noticed a sudden lilt in Belle's voice. "I'm sure he wouldn't mind seeing you."

Delta lowered The Fuzz's foot and slowly straightened her spine. "I never figured you would be one to play Cupid."

"Who's playing Cupid?"

Delta lifted one brow and cleared her throat.

"Okay, so maybe I am. Can you blame me? You two would be good for each other. You're both single."

"Yeah, well you're forgetting two things." Delta lifted the horse's foot again and examined it. No further cracks, but the outside was still slightly asymmetrical. "He's still grieving his wife and I'm happily divorced."

"I never knew you were married." Belle pulled a carrot from her pocket and fed it to the horse. "I guess it didn't end well, huh?"

"You think?" Delta glanced up at her. "Thanks but no thanks. I don't date clients."

"He said that, too."

"Garrett did?" She lowered the hoof. "Wait a minute. Have you also suggested us dating to him?"

"I may have mentioned it the other night...and the week before." Belle looked skyward. "But Harlan started it. Well, actually, Dylan. They both thought you two were seeing each other."

"Why would they—" Then the realization hit her. This was why dating in a small town was next to impossible. Everyone knew your business. "It was just dinner."

Delta returned her attention to The Fuzz and lifted his foot for the third time, determined to finish it.

"He's a really great guy," Belle said under her breath.

Delta chose to ignore the comment. If she didn't engage her, maybe she'd drop the conversation.

"I'm just saying," Belle added. "Wouldn't it be nice to have someone to go to the movies with or take little day trips with?"

"My day trips consist of driving hom—back to Missoula to visit my family, and I'm not big on the movie theatre." So much for not engaging her. "Even if I was, I have friends I could call. I don't need a man to complete me."

"But don't you want one to share your life with?"

"If and when the right man comes along, I will consider it." She lowered the horse's hoof. "But Garrett is not that person. He's not ready. And neither you, or Harlan, or anyone can determine when he will be. He'll know when the time is right. So put your arrows back in their quiver, Miss Cupid."

"Okay." Belle rested her head against the horse's neck, making it almost impossible to tell where her platinum hair ended and his light mane began. "But please think about seeing Kacey."

"That I'll do." She needed to swing by Silver Bells to check on Lightning Bug anyway. "I'll pick up Jake early from BowWowWowzer's and go today. I'm sure he'd love to see her, too."

She was only doing this for Kacey. It had nothing to do with wanting to see how Garrett was handling everything. Her parents had blamed themselves when it had happened to Delta. It wasn't always easy to ask for help as a kid. And at the time, a part of her blamed them, too. How could they not have known she was in so much pain? But she had done everything in her power to hide it from them and her brothers.

As an adult, she understood both sides of the equation. Okay, so maybe she could bend her friend rule and offer some comfort to Garrett. If she could just manage to keep her heart out of it, she'd be fine. Delta sensed another test of her will coming on and she wasn't so sure she'd pass this one. She wasn't Wonder Woman. She didn't have a shield to protect her. And Lord knew she needed one against Garrett Slade.

Chapter Six

Jake barreled down the stable corridor toward Kacey. Garrett hadn't seen her smile that big in—he didn't know how long. His daughter knelt on the floor and wrapped her arms around the dog's neck, burying her face in his long blue merle coat. He glanced toward the entrance, but didn't see Delta. If Jake was there, she had to be somewhere nearby.

"Daddy, where's Delta?"

"I'm sure she'll be in shortly."

When fifteen minutes had passed, Garrett's concern grew. Where was she? Could Jake have gotten away from her and run to the stables? He told himself not to worry, but lately it was all he did.

"Sweetheart, you stay here with Jake. I'll be right back."

Garrett's strides lengthened as he headed for the door. He swung it wide and saw Delta lying on the ground, next to her truck.

"Delta!" he shouted as he ran to her.

She scurried to her feet, holding a long pipe like a Samurai warrior. "What?" She glanced around her. "What is it? What did Jake do?"

"He's fine. He's with Kacey. I saw you lying on the ground. Are you all right?"

She rubbed her forehead, leaving behind a dirt-streak. He fought the urge to wipe it away. The last thing he needed was to come in contact with her skin, which he imagined was silkier than silk itself.

"I am, but I can't say the same for my tire." Delta stepped to the side. "I knew something didn't feel right when I was parking. My jack keeps slipping so I can't raise it enough to change the damn thing. Getting a new jack has been on my list for months and I never do anything about it."

Garrett crouched next to her truck and saw two nails sticking out of the tire. Probably courtesy of the renovations they had been doing on the ranch's outbuildings. "Let me change it for you. I'll pay for your new tire, too. This is our fault. I told those guys to go over the ground with a magnet to pick up all the nails. Not just for the cars, but for the horses and our guests. I don't need someone or something impaled on a nail."

"I appreciate that, but I've been all over the place today so I could've picked those up anywhere. All I need right now is a heavy-duty jack. You wouldn't happen to have one around here, would you?"

"Yep. I have one in the barn." Garrett hadn't noticed the flecks of gold in her eyes before. They reminded him of a piece of amber he'd found as a child. Alluring yet mysterious.

"Um, if you tell me where in the barn—"

"I'm sorry. My mind was elsewhere for a second." Garrett stepped around her, careful not to accidentally brush against her body. "Let me go get it. And don't argue with me... I'm changing that tire."

Delta held up her hands in surrender. "Okay. My bones are aching from working this week anyway, so be my guest."

Garrett enjoyed the sight of a woman who didn't mind getting her hands dirty. Probably too much so where Delta was concerned. It didn't help that the woman smelled dark and delicious. As if that was even a scent. He still couldn't pin down what she was wearing. A woman who worked around horses all day should smell like horse. And hay. He would even settle for manure. Anything to distract him from the allure that had begun to draw him toward her. He had Belle and Harlan to thank for that. Every time Kacey had mentioned Delta's name over the past week, they had taken every opportunity to remind him she was single.

A half hour later, Garrett let the jack down and removed it from under her truck. "You're all set. Please let me take your tire into town so I can get a new one put on this rim."

She stepped closer to him. "You don't have to do that. I'll just have it patched."

"Nonsense." Garrett swore he could feel the heat emanating off her body in the cold Montana afternoon. "You, uh—you do way too much traveling to ride around on a patched tire, especially with a truck this size." Garrett reached for the tire and began rolling it toward his truck. "I'm not going to discuss it further," he called over his shoulder, grateful for the distance between them. "I'm getting you a new tire and I'll have it back to you on Monday."

"Absolutely not." Delta ran to block him, causing Garrett to slam into her and push them both against the bed of his truck. He grabbed her waist to steady her, allowing the tire to wobble to the ground. Delta's lush, full lips were inches from his as they parted slightly. As she inhaled, her breasts pressed against his chest, sending his mind in numerous directions. "But, I will take you up on your dinner offer, if it still stands."

Garrett tried to open his mouth to speak but feared any movement he made would be toward her, especially toward kissing her.

"Garrett." Her hands wrapped around his, which were now resting on her hips. "Did you hear me?"

"Ye— I— Yeah— Yes!" Garrett released her and took a step back, tripping over the tire instead.

"Watch out!" Delta grabbed hold of his arm and steadied him before he hit the ground. "Don't you go falling head over boots."

Too late.

"I'm good." He lifted the tire and set it in his truck bed. "This is coming with me." He grabbed two bungee cords from his cab and began to tie the tire in place. If he kept his hands busy, they wouldn't wind up back on her. "So, what's this about dinner?"

"I heard what you had said and maybe I have been a little too rigid with my rules. Dinner with a friend never hurt anyone."

Garrett looked up just as she tucked her hair behind one ear, exposing the delicate side of her neck. It was one of his favorite places to kiss on a woman's body. Well, Rebecca's body. He'd never been with anyone else. That fact alone was enough to temper his libido.

Despite his attraction to Delta, if it came down to it, he wouldn't be able to follow through. He couldn't betray Rebecca that way.

"Harlan and Belle are taking the kids this weekend. We have a little arrangement going on. Why don't we go over there?" *Safety in numbers*, Garret thought to himself.

"I was thinking someplace a little more private. Where we could talk…alone."

Garrett's pulse quickened. "Isn't that living a little too dangerously? You're just tossing all your rules out the window."

"This has nothing to do with rules." Delta inched closer as he jumped from the truck bed. "It has everything to do with you and what happened with Kacey. I can relate to how she's feeling. But I also understand how you're feeling because I watched my parents go through the same thing."

Garrett couldn't deny wanting to talk to her about Kacey. He had picked up the phone repeatedly during the week and set it back down, uncertain how to ask her to relive a painful time in her life just to give him some peace of mind.

"I'd like to get your input on the situation, if you're sure it won't bring up too many bad memories."

"Undoubtedly it will, but the more I thought about it, the more I realized you need a friend who's been there. I want to help you, if I can. Heck, maybe if we spend some time together, Belle and Harlan will lay off the matchmaking. With Valentine's Day coming up, maybe we can duck and dodge Saddle Ridge's cupids together."

Her idea wasn't half bad. It would keep his brothers

at bay. He wasn't so sure about Belle, but it might work. "Sounds like a plan."

"Great. Oh, and as for my tire, I'm going to deduct the price of a new one off your next invoice." She lifted her chin defiantly.

Garrett laughed. He should have known it wouldn't be that simple. "You'll do no such thing."

"Oh, please, you'll never even know. I'll just leave something off an invoice and you won't be the wiser."

"Are you challenging me?" Garrett watched her draw her bottom lip inward, renewing every urge to kiss her.

"Daddy, what time are we going to Uncle Harlan's?"

Garrett stepped back from Delta and clenched his fists. That was close. Too close. He was a fool for thinking of kissing her, even for a second. "Not for a few more—"

"Delta!" Kacey ran down the walkway with Jake in tow and threw herself into Delta's arms. "I missed you."

"You missed me?" She looked at Garrett questioningly as she hugged his daughter.

He shrugged, surprised at Kacey's attachment to someone she'd only met once.

"I wondered when I would see you again. Daddy, can Delta come with us tonight?"

"Oh, honey. You don't put someone on the spot like that." He wanted to spare Delta having to say no to his daughter.

"Your father just asked me the same thing. I would love to." Delta smiled up at him and shrugged. "How could I possibly turn down an invite from you?"

"Yay!" Kacey jumped up and down. "Can Jake come, too?"

"I don't know about that." Delta laughed nervously. "I think one extra guest for dinner is enough. Jake's been at doggy daycare all morning so I'm sure he won't mind staying home and catching up on his beauty sleep tonight." She held Kacey by the shoulders and lowered her face to hers. "I'll tell you what, though, you are welcome to play with Jake whenever you want. If it's okay with your father, I'll give you my number so you can call me and we'll set up a playdate."

"Did you hear that, Daddy?" Kacey tugged at his arm. "It's okay, isn't it?"

It was more than all right. If Delta could make his daughter this happy by allowing her to spend time with Jake, she could move in for all he cared. "Sounds good to me."

"We're going to have playdates, Jake." The dog jumped up and down on his hind legs in front of Kacey and if he didn't know better, he'd swear the animal understood what they were saying.

Kacey stopped jumping and ran over to Delta's rear passenger-side window. She climbed on the running boards and pressed her face against the glass. "Is that a guitar?" She expectantly looked at Delta for a response. "Do you play?"

"Yes."

"Are you in a band? Can you teach me to play?"

Delta threw her head back and laughed. "I'm not in a band. But I do bring it with me to the convalescent home here in town. Sometimes when I visit the people there, they ask me to sing songs for them."

"What is a con-con-val—"

"Convalescent. It's a nursing home." Kacey didn't

realize it, but she had been to one before. Rebecca had spent two months in one before they brought her home to die. Garrett swallowed hard. "People stay there when they need 24-hour care. Delta goes there to cheer them up. If you want to learn how to play guitar, I'm sure Dylan will teach you."

"I want Delta to teach me." She turned away from him. "Can I go with you to the con-va-scent home?"

Garrett didn't want his daughter visiting a nursing home. Not this close to the anniversary of her mother's death.

"Not tonight, honey." Delta seemed to sense his anxiety. "Jake and I wanted to stop in and see you and Lightning Bug and then I need to shower and get cleaned up. I'll stop by the home and then I will meet you both for dinner. When is dinner? I don't want to be late."

"Not until seven, seven-thirty. By the time Harlan gets home from work and I get out of here and clean up myself, and then wrangle my two, it takes us a while to sit down and eat."

"Sounds perfect." Delta wrapped an arm around Kacey's shoulders and began walking toward the stables as Jake fell into step beside them. "How would you like to help me examine Lightning Bug's foot."

"I'd like that." Kacey wound her arm around Delta's waist in return. "You still didn't say if you would teach me guitar or not."

"If your father says yes, then I will." She turned to him. "I wouldn't mind at all."

"Daddy, can I?" Kacey's doe-eyed expression made it impossible to refuse.

"If Delta is willing to teach you, sure." Garrett had

been trying to think of the perfect birthday gift for his daughter. He had already considered a puppy, but now he was thinking about a puppy and a guitar. Were his ears ready for that kind of assault? If it made her happy again, he didn't care. He'd like to see his daughter stick with something. She bored easily and he didn't know if that had been because of the somber environment they had been living in or if she genuinely hadn't found something she really cared about. Maybe animals and music would be her thing.

"Thank you, Daddy." Kacey ran over and gave him a quick hug before running back to Delta and grabbing her hand. "I can't wait to tell Ivy."

"I heard you're in a new school." Delta unlatched Lightning Bug's door and stepped inside while Kacey climbed up on a hay bale and watched her through the stall bars. "How do you like it?"

"It's okay." Kacey shrugged. "I still haven't learned everyone's names yet."

"Yeah, that's always hard," Delta said as Garrett sank farther into the shadows of the tack room doorway. A part of him felt like he was spying on his daughter. The other part felt if he had done more spying, she never would have been bullied to the extent she had been. "I went through that when I went to a new school, too."

"You did?" Kacey lifted her head.

"Things were a little different back then. They didn't kick my bullies out of school like they did yours. All they did was move us to different classes, which didn't help on the playground, so my parents put me in a private school, too."

"Did you like it?" Kacey asked.

"Not at first. I was scared. And like you, I didn't know anyone. But the teachers were nice and the kids were even nicer. Some of my best friends to this day were from that school."

"Really?"

"Yep. It's just like when I moved here from Missoula and started a new job. I knew one person in town. I had to start all over again. And you know what? It was so much harder as an adult than it was as a kid. At least when I was your age, I had classmates to talk to and get to know. Here I had to go out to strange places and make a point of meeting people. I was nervous."

"You were?"

"Oh, yeah. But I did it, and I have some great friends here, too."

"Like Daddy?"

Delta paused. "Your daddy and I are getting to know one another a little better."

"Are you still nervous around him?"

Now there was a question he wanted answered himself. He leaned farther into the corridor to hear Delta's response, but of course she wouldn't make it easy on him. The two had taken to whispering like two schoolgirls. Curiosity be damned, he was just happy Delta got his daughter talking freely about school. She hadn't been as forthright with him. The woman may pose a serious risk to his heart, but she was good for Kacey. And her needs came before his. As long as he kept all of *his* wants and needs where Delta was concerned in check, he'd survive.

THE FOLLOWING NIGHT, Delta stood in front of her open closet door and stared into the emptiness. She had nothing left to wear. *It's just dinner.* Then why was she nervous? *It's just dinner.* For the second night in a row.

She turned to the mound of clothes on the bed and sighed. She had tried everything on. Twice. And she still couldn't decide what to wear tonight. Yesterday had been easy. They had gone to Harlan and Belle's with the kids. That was a jeans-and-sweater-type event. One she had enjoyed more than she'd anticipated.

Oh, and that Bryce. She just wanted to eat him up. He had such a cherub face, with pink rosy cheeks, beautiful blue eyes and white-blond hair. That was how she pictured Rebecca. She had no idea what the woman looked like, but that image had come to mind before she'd even met Bryce. She and Garrett had created two beautiful children.

And Delta needed to remember that.

Garrett was in love with Rebecca. There would never be anything more than friendship between him and Delta. She grabbed the empty hangers from the closet and began plucking items off the bed one by one. Black jeans, a pale blue denim shirt and her leather motorcycle jacket. There. Done.

It's just dinner. With a friend. On a Saturday night.

Delta arrived at the Iron Horse Bar & Grill ten minutes before six and parked her red hardtop Jeep Wrangler near the entrance. It was still a bit too early for the evening crowd and she figured she'd be able to get them a table near the bar so they wouldn't risk being stuck in a dark, cozy corner booth. Probably a booth he had shared with Rebecca when they were younger. Knowing Garrett's history with the place, she was surprised when he had suggested it. Then again, maybe that was why he had. It was someplace old and familiar, a place guaranteed to remind him of what he'd had and lost.

She walked in the door and was immediately hit in the chest by Cupid's arrow. *Seriously?* She stared at the foam arrow lying on the floor.

A rather attractive twentysomething cowboy with piercing blue eyes knelt before her. Her breath caught in her throat until he opened his mouth. "I'm so sorry, ma'am. My aim is way off tonight." Then he retrieved the arrow and joined the rest of his pretty twentysomething friends.

Ma'am? You've got to be kidding me. The one place she thought had escaped the Valentine fervor had transformed their game area into Cupid's lair. The pitch penny bench was covered in red leather. Giant diapered cherub butts covered the dartboards that people shot foam and Velcro arrows at and the Cornhole platforms had been painted red and had baskets of red and white beanbags next to them. At least they had left the billiard tables untouched.

She sighed and turned to find a table when she saw Garrett waving to her. So much for her arriving first. He wasn't quite in the dark corner she had feared, but it was the next booth over. Booths were intimate. Especially at the Iron Horse. It was where you brought your date after a movie or before a night of dancing. It wasn't a hey-let's-talk-about-horseshoes type of table.

Garrett stood and removed his hat as she approached. "You look nice tonight," he said as she slid into her side of the booth. "I hope this is okay?"

"Thank you and it's perfect." She couldn't help admiring the snug cut of his jeans and the way they hugged every single curve of his body. And the man had curves. He didn't have those straight, spindly legs that some men had. He had very defined muscular thighs with…bulges. Garrett Slade had nice bulges. "You look nice, too."

And he did once he sat down and his bulges were out of her direct line of sight. He had on a fawn-colored flannel shirt that made her want to snuggle against it. She could just imagine what it would feel like to be enveloped in his arms with her face pressed against his chest.

Shirt. Her face pressed against his shirt.

Nope. That didn't work either. She didn't need to be pressing any of her parts against any of his. If he hadn't cleaned up so well, these thoughts wouldn't be invading her brain. And it wasn't as if she'd ever seen Garrett get really dirty. The man changed her truck tire and barely got anything on him. He was rugged. He had an air of I'm-ready-to-get-dirty-at-any-moment quality about him, but there was always a flicker of something mischievous behind his dark eyes.

"I ordered us two chipotle whiskeys and a couple of beers. I hope you don't mind."

"Oh no, definitely don't mind." A drink couldn't come fast enough. "What's with the Valentine's Day onslaught when you walk in the door?"

"I was going to ask you the same thing." He leaned closer so she could hear him over the music, bringing with him a heady scent of woodsy aftershave. *Lord help me he smells good.* "It's bad enough I have to deal with this stuff at the ranch."

"The ranch does Valentine's Day? I don't remember that last year."

"It's all Emma's fault. Her wedding planning with Dylan is turning everything into one big Silver Bells lovefest."

Delta tried not to laugh but the way he said *lovefest* looked like he'd swallowed a pinch of chewing tobacco.

"I'm serious." He leaned back as the waitress set their drinks on the table between them. "We have a week-long Valentine's couples-only retreat coming up and it's making everyone in an amorous mood up at the lodge. Thank God my job is in the stables. I don't even go up there for breakfast anymore. Considering half our employees are married to each other, everyone is hand holding or sneaking in a kiss here and there. We're running a business, not a lover's playground."

"Remind me not to step foot in there until that's over with." She raised her whiskey glass. "Here's to avoiding Valentine's Day."

"I'll drink to that." Garrett clinked her glass.

Waylon Jennings' "Good Hearted Woman" played on the jukebox and Delta found herself itching to get on the dance floor. If it had been any other place with any other man, she would have. She looked up at Garrett, fully expecting him to be lost in his memories of what once was. Instead, his eyes met hers and he smiled.

"You want to dance, don't you?"

"No, I'm good." The truth was, she had been wiped out most of the day. Work had been a struggle, but somewhere around four o'clock, she found her second wind. "Kicking back with good company and good food is about all I can handle tonight."

"Long day?"

"Busy. Many small jobs all over the county. What about you? How are renovations going?"

"I wish I had more to do with them." Garrett flipped open his menu. "Dylan's acting general contractor and I'm maintaining status quo in the stables. Thanks to Belle's help, I've managed to barter some construction services in exchange for riding lessons and a few free stays at the ranch once the cabins are finished."

"That's a great idea."

"It's managing to save us more than I had expected, but that's been the extent of my involvement. My brother runs all the ideas past me and we decide on them together, but I always get the feeling he thinks I'll break if he gives me too much work to do. I want to do more. Our staff is thin, but it's also winter. I can easily appoint someone to manage the stables while I work with Dylan. But he won't give."

"Working with family can be tough." Delta sipped at her whiskey. "When I worked for my dad, I never thought I'd make it out of apprentice mode. Even after I had become a journeyman, I still felt like I was apprenticing under him."

"It dawned on me the other day who your father is. I hadn't put two and two together before. Luther Lloyd Grace is a legend. He's a master blacksmith, too, isn't he?"

"Don't ever let him hear you call him by his real name. Luther Lloyd makes him cringe. You be sure to call him Buck. And yes, he is a master blacksmith. You know the man, you know the legend that is the man, and how could I complain about working under someone with his world-renowned expertise? It's also a hell of a lot to live up to when you're the only kid who followed in his footsteps."

After four generations of Grace farriers, she was also where the legend ended, since she couldn't have kids of her own. One of her brothers worked for the Missoula County Sheriff's Department and the other was a Montana Travler horse breeder. Even if they had kids of their own and they chose to become farriers, it would have skipped a generation.

Her father and grandfather had been so proud to pass the torch, and then her body betrayed her by single-handedly snuffing it out. Her father would never admit to his disappointment, but she knew it was there. A few months ago, she'd overheard him trying to convince Trevor to stop breeding horses and apprentice under him. He hadn't given any reasons. He hadn't had to. But she knew. They all knew.

"Can I offer you a piece of advice?" she asked.

"Sure." Garrett sipped at his whiskey. "This stuff is pretty good once you get used to it."

"I'm glad to see that lesson stuck with you."

He leaned forward on the table and smiled a slow easy grin that caused her heart to skip a beat. "Give me your advice."

Delta rolled her shoulders. She didn't know if it was the man or the heat of the whiskey that made her feel deliciously warm. "Be honest with your brother. If you want more, tell him. He may think he's doing you a favor. Once I told my dad I wanted my own business, he supported me. And when Henry called and told him about Saddle Ridge, he practically pushed me out the door. You might be surprised at his reaction."

"You know what, I will do just that. Tomorrow. Tonight is about friendship."

He raised his pint of Guinness.

"To friendship." She clinked her glass against his.

"And ice skating."

"And what now?" Delta froze before the dark liquid touched her lips. "I am not drinking to that."

"Why not?" Garrett frowned. "The rink is a few blocks down and I thought we could pop over there after dinner."

"The only popping would be my butt bouncing across the ice. I do not skate. I've tried it and I'm not good at it. And no amount of lessons will help me either. I've already gone down that slippery path."

"I didn't think there was anything Delta Grace couldn't do."

"Yeah, well. We all have our limitations."

"HOLD ON TO my hands." Delta hadn't been kidding when she'd said she couldn't skate. The woman could barely stand. "I've got you."

"I cannot believe you talked me into this." Her eyes narrowed at him. "This is not my idea of a good time. What if we fall through?"

"Then you'll be standing in an inch of water." He skated backwards, pulling her with him. "We're skating on a parking lot. It freezes quickly when the temps drop. I promise you won't fall through the ice and drown."

"Oh, you're funny."

"Where's that confidence I know you have?" Garrett

enjoyed challenging Delta. She was a little bit of a bad girl mixed with a little bit of sweet. Once he cracked through her hard exterior, he enjoyed getting to know her softer side.

"If I fall—"

"I'll catch you."

"Forget that. I don't want you to catch me. If I fall, you owe me ten more dinners."

"Such a hardship. I don't know if I can handle that."

"Daddy!" a tiny voice called from behind him. "Look, Belle. It's Daddy and Delta."

He dropped Delta's hands when he turned to see Kacey skating toward them.

"What the—erm— Ow."

"Delta!" Kacey skidded to a stop beside Delta sitting on the ice. "Daddy, why did you let go of her?"

"Yeah, Garrett?" Delta snarled. "Why did you let go of me."

"I—I…give me your hand." He reached for her, but she refused to budge. He hadn't meant to drop her. Kacey startled him and he didn't want her to get the wrong idea. He didn't think Delta would fall that fast. Or that hard. "I'm sorry, really I am."

"Go away." She swatted at him.

"Lean on me, Delta. I'll help you," Kacey said.

"No, honey, if I fall again—and I'm sure I will—I don't want to crush you. I am not a skater."

"Sure you are." Belle's arms slid under hers from behind and within seconds, Delta was standing on her feet. "What do you say, Kacey? How about we teach her how the Slade girls skate. Come on, Ivy."

"Yeah!" Kacey grabbed hold of one hand and Belle

the other and off they went gliding over the ice at warp speed while Ivy skated in front of the team cheering them on.

"I bet you five this doesn't end well." Harlan held out a gloved hand.

"Nah, I think she'll get it. She just needed the right teacher. She wasn't born on the ice like our kids." Bryce skated around them.

"First dinner last night at my house, and then tonight we find you out here together. Balk all you want, but whatever is going on between you two looks like a relationship to me."

Leave it to the deputy sheriff to dig for information. Hey, at least if he and Belle suspected they were dating, they'd lay off the matchmaking.

"We went out to dinner and then I talked her into coming here."

"Slow down," Delta cried as they flew by. "You're going too fast."

"Open your eyes and move your feet," Kacey ordered. "It's the only way you're going to learn."

The men started to laugh. "You can see how well that worked out for me."

"You're skating, Delta," Ivy shouted.

"Well, I'll be damned," Garrett said. "She is skating." With Belle's and Kacey's help. But she was skating nonetheless.

"Daddy, look at Delta." The women slowed to a stop in front of Harlan, Bryce and Garrett.

"See, we knew you could do it." Belle nudged Delta's arm. "All it took was a Slade to open your eyes."

There was no hiding the double meaning of that

statement. But it had also been a Slade who allowed her to fall because he didn't want to risk his daughter seeing them together. Delta's reaction afterward told him there was no hiding that meaning either.

"You're a better teacher than I am, sweetie." Garrett flicked the pompom on his daughter's hat.

"Ain't that the truth." Delta stuck out her tongue at him, making the girls giggle.

"Daddy, do you think you can manage to skate with Delta again, and not let her fall? Or do I have to supervise?"

"Oh, snap!" Delta laughed. "She told you."

"I guess she did." If Kacey didn't have a problem with them skating together, then why should he? He bowed before Delta and extended his hand. "May I have this skate?"

"Do you promise not to let go?"

Kacey joined their hands together. "He promises."

"I promise. I won't let go." And he didn't for the rest of their time on the ice. Belle and Harlan had left long before they did. The hour had gotten away from Garrett, and when they stepped off the ice when the rink shut off the lights for the night, Garrett found himself fighting the urge to kiss Delta good-night as they walked back to where they had parked.

"I guess I owe you ten more dinners."

"I guess you do." Delta opened her truck door. "Thanks again for tonight," she said before climbing in.

"It was my pleasure. Drive safe." He patted the hood of her Jeep as she backed out of the space. He stood on the curb and watched her taillights disappear into the night. Tonight had been more fun than he had anticipated. And much lonelier than he could have ever imagined. There was no one waiting for him at home. No wife, no kids. Just emptiness. And in that moment, he wished he hadn't let Delta drive away.

Chapter Seven

Delta awoke Sunday morning to a head on her shoulder
and a hot breath against her cheek. She glanced at the
clock on the nightstand. It wasn't even six in the morning and she didn't have anywhere to be. Days like these
were a rare treat. Normally she had jobs lined up, or if
she had gone to visit her parents, she would be driving
home. Today her schedule was clear and it was hers to
do as she pleased.

The body next to her shifted and yawned, followed
by a long lazy stretch and a paw to the face. "Easy with
the right hook there, bud." Jake's breathing deepened
until it became a steady snore. "And Belle thinks I need
a man to share my life with. I don't need a man. I have
Jake." Between his gas and snoring, he was as close to
a man as she wanted to get.

Delta smiled, remembering last night with Garrett.
It had been completely unexpected and more fun than
she thought it would be. At the end of the night, she had
thought he was about to kiss her. He didn't, and she still
wasn't quite sure how she felt about that.

She sat up in bed and looked around the room, realizing she didn't know how to start her day without an

alarm clock ringing in her ear. She should be enjoying her day off and sleeping in, but her body betrayed her. Swinging her legs over the side, Delta groaned as she stood. Between the muscle aches and stiff joints, she felt a hundred years old. Who knew ice skating for hours would hurt so much the next day?

She padded downstairs and filled the coffee carafe with water. Her parents had given her one of those single-serve coffeemakers for Christmas, but it was still sitting in the box on top of her dryer in the laundry room. She was a creature of habit and her habit was making a thermos of coffee every morning and taking it with her. But, she wasn't going anywhere and she certainly didn't need a thermos of caffeine to do nothing.

"What the heck." She walked into the laundry room, picked up the box and sat it on the kitchen table. Today was a good day to change things up.

An hour later, Delta was on caffeine overload. It was her mother's fault. She had included six different kinds of coffee with the gift and Delta had to try them all. After she showered and dressed, it was still only seven thirty in the morning.

"What do people do with all their free time?" She didn't exactly have any hobbies. There was guitar, but sitting around the house didn't appeal to her today. It was too early to call Liv or Maddie. Even the convalescent home frowned on visitors until after nine o'clock. And it was too cold to go for a hike. "What are we going to do, Jake?"

She stared at her phone, willing a customer to call… willing Garrett to call. And that wasn't right. He didn't need to call her. He had no business calling her. Unless of course, it was for business. Try as she might, she couldn't get him off her mind. It didn't help that he had held her hand while they skated. She hadn't had that kind of intimate contact with anyone since her husband and she missed it, but she certainly didn't miss him.

The man she had spent most of her life loving couldn't handle what the chemotherapy had done to her body. It hadn't just been the hair loss or the constant sickness. It had been the harsh reality that she may not survive. And even if she did, knowing they'd never conceive a child together had driven a huge wedge between them. The turmoil they had experienced was common. Many marriages went through it. There were support groups, but Eddie had refused to attend a single meeting. Regardless of how strong their love had been, it hadn't been strong enough.

If he had told her he wanted to end the marriage she would have still been devastated, but she would've respected his honesty. Instead, he had chosen the coward's way out by distancing himself from her and having an affair with a mutual friend of theirs. Some friend. While Delta fought for her life, Eddie had knocked up his girlfriend. Her world had collapsed around her and she had lost the will to fight. Until Jake.

The dog nudged her knee with his nose, sensing her tension. "What is it, boy? You're bored, too, huh? Come on, let's take a ride into town and see what trouble we can get into."

Delta zipped her ski jacket to the top of the collar. She wished the weather would make up its mind. This morning had to be thirty degrees colder than yesterday afternoon. Jake ran ahead of her and waited patiently by the passenger door of her work truck.

"Not today. We're going in the Jeep." Without hesitation, Jake ran to that vehicle and waited for her by the other passenger door. His intelligence scared her sometimes. "How about we pick you up some dog food?" she asked as he jumped onto the seat.

The only place dog-friendly at that hour of the morning was Saddle Ridge Feed & Tack. She wasn't out of food yet, but she would be by the end of the week. Apparently, half the town had the same idea because the parking lot was almost full. Jake sat still so she could snap a leash on his collar before they stepped out of the Jeep.

A blast of hot air from the heater above the automatic double doors instantly dried her eyes as they entered the store. Jake trotted happily by her side, scanning the floor for bits and pieces of kibble and grain that inadvertently fell out of bags when people brought them up to the register.

"I have a bone to pick with you, Miss Grace," a man said from behind as they were turning down the dog food aisle.

"I beg your pardon." The hair on the back of her neck rose as she spun on him. Garrett. He glared at her with his arms folded across his chest and a scowl the size of Montana plastered across his face. "Oh, hey." Garrett's expression didn't change, nor did he move. "Okay, I'll bite. Why do you have a bone to pick with me?"

"I took your advice, and I spoke to my brother this morning."

"Judging by the look, I'm assuming your conversation fell on deaf ears."

"Oh, no." Garrett tilted back his hat. "Dylan thought it was a great idea."

"So that's good, right?" Garrett shook his head. "It's not good?" Delta wasn't following.

"He put me in charge of the Valentine's week couples-only retreat I told you about last night."

"Ew." Delta wouldn't want that job. "I don't understand. Why isn't Emma planning the retreat? I thought she was running the guest lodge."

"Her daughter's only four weeks old and Emma's not ready to work full-time yet. She's been handling all the marketing from home. She got local TV and radio stations to advertise the retreat in exchange for placing their advertising on our revamped website. Plus, she's planning a wedding. So instead of Dylan putting me in charge of the lodge and having her work on this, they thought it would be great for me to organize all the events, work with the chefs on creating the menus and sprucing the place up so it looks more romantic. All on a tight budget."

"Don't take this the wrong way, Garrett, but you don't exactly scream Mr. Romance." Delta carefully chose her words, not wanting to add insult to injury. "Let's put it this way, a couples-only retreat requires a more feminine touch. I'd think Emma would want to handle that herself."

"I got the impression Dylan's afraid she might make things too sophisticated. It wasn't all that long ago when her plans for the ranch involved turning it into a high-end resort."

"I remember your uncle Jax telling me about that. I never could envision those changes for Silver Bells."

"Neither could Dylan, which is why he fought so hard to keep it. This event is a soft reopening of sorts." Garrett rubbed the back of his neck. "We haven't had any bookings since the first of the year, since Jax had planned to sell the ranch. His death threw everything into a frenzy. Emma sent out a newsletter to everyone on our mailing list to let them know we weren't closing, but we don't reopen until February 1. This Valentine's event sets the tone for the couples-only vacation packages we plan to start offering."

"All the more reason for you not to handle it."

"This retreat has to appeal to men and women. Silver Bells has always been a family guest ranch and that's great in the summer. Newer ranches took a huge chunk of our business. The romantic getaway aspect would be something they don't have, especially when most of our competition is closed during the winter months."

"I still don't see where you come in."

"Emma's goal is to add at least one couples-only week or weekend a month depending on the time of year, but if we don't appeal to the male client, the concept fails. Dylan doesn't want to contradict his soon-to-be wife's ideas, so he put me in charge to eliminate them from the equation. Much to Emma's dismay."

"That's a lot to take on alone. Can't you get somebody there to help you?"

"Oh, somebody's going to be helping me. You."

"Me? Why me?" Delta held up her hands in protest. She refused to play any part of someone else's romantic vacation. "I hate Valentine's Day."

"Yeah, you and me both. Your advice got me into this mess and you're going to help me clean it up. That's what friends are for."

"Garrett, I don't have a romantic bone in my body." He'd have better luck with Jake helping him.

"Well, you better find one. You better find lots of romantic bones because I don't have a lot of time to get everything planned and ordered before February 10 when the retreat begins. We already have regular guests coming in a few days from now."

Delta quickly did the math in her head. "The tenth is only two weeks from now."

"It sure is, sweetheart. So—" Garrett wrapped his arm around her shoulder. "What are your plans for the rest of the day?"

"Apparently, I'm planning a romantic Valentine's retreat with you." She forced a smile. "I just have to pick up a few things and then I will meet you in your office."

"Make it my house. I'd like at least one day away from my office. The kids won't be home until later tonight and we'll have room to spread out. If we need to go up to the lodge, we can. I'll wait and you can follow me home."

Great. Delta hefted a bag of dog food into her arms. Just what she needed. Being alone, in a house, with a man she was trying to convince herself not to fall for. Her and her big mouth.

GARRETT CHECKED THE rearview mirror to make sure Delta was still following him and hadn't decided to make a break for it. Not that he could blame her. He didn't know any sane single person who would want to plan for a couples-only Valentine's retreat. And it irked him that Dylan even thought this was a good idea.

He didn't want to think about Valentine's Day. He didn't want to think about love and romance. He didn't want to think. He just wanted to do *real* ranch work. Hard work that left him too tired to think at the end of the day. That had been part of the reasoning behind moving to Saddle Ridge.

Silver Bells had offered him a clean slate. Rebecca had visited Jax's house and the lodge, but she'd never been in this house. He didn't picture her sitting on his couch or lying in his loft bedroom. He didn't see her standing at the kitchen sink or having dinner at the table. His home was Rebecca free and that hurt equally as much as his need for that freedom.

He parked in front of the house and waited for Delta and Jake. He wanted to make a joke about the mission they were about to embark upon, but his mouth became cottony dry as they climbed the front steps. Maybe taking her to his house wasn't such a hot idea. There wasn't anything wrong with two friends working on a project together, because they were just friends.

Just. Friends.

Yep, that was why he'd almost kissed her at the skating rink. And guilt from that had kept him up most of the night. It didn't matter that Rebecca had given him her blessing to move on after she was gone. It felt like a betrayal. And he was a fool for even thinking Delta would want anything romantic to do with him. She was single and beautiful. She could have any man she wanted in town. She was also standoffish. The reality was, he didn't know anything about her beyond her dog and her working for the ranch. He sensed she had a story to tell. There had to be some reason she didn't like mixing friendship with work. It was an extreme response. And Garrett knew all about extreme.

He silently held the front door open for her. She white-knuckle gripped Jake's leash as she cautiously stepped inside, as if uncertain what she might find. He had spent a few hours cleaning up last night, trying to burn off his guilt. The house bordered on spotless, his conscience on the other hand did not.

He closed the door behind them and hung his hat on the hook beside it. "I hadn't thought to ask if you had eaten yet. We could've stopped somewhere on the way and picked up something to bring back. Or I can fix breakfast. If you're okay with bacon, eggs and toast. It's about all I have. Unless you're a vegan like Belle and Ivy, then I can offer you toast and blueberry jam. Or, if you'd like something else, I can run back into town."

Delta and Jake stood frozen in the middle of his living room staring at him with their mouths open. Jake looked up at Delta and then to Garrett and back. She unclipped his leash and nodded. The dog crossed the room and sat in front of him, before lifting his paw and waving. He couldn't help but smile at the gesture. He knelt in front of Jake and scratched the dog behind both ears.

"You did that on purpose, didn't you?" he asked Delta.

"You needed to breathe." She smiled warmly at him. There was no judgment. No fear. Just friendship. And that meant everything right now.

"Thank you. I know this might sound weird but

you're the first non-relative female to come into my home."

"Nah, it's not weird. I get it. I've been divorced for almost three years and I still haven't had a man over to my place. Friend or otherwise. What you're feeling is normal. Believe it or not, we're normal."

Now there was something he hadn't known. She'd been married before. And divorced. That must be the bad breakup she'd mentioned their first night together at the Iron Horse.

"Speak for yourself. I haven't felt normal in years." He stood and walked to her. "Here, let me take your jacket, unless you want to get something to eat in town."

"Whatever you're more comfortable with. But by the time we drive there and back we would probably waste over an hour or more. I'm brave enough to try your cooking." She eased out of her jacket and handed it to him. "What can I help you with, because I insist on helping."

"How about you start on the eggs while I defrost the bacon." Garrett led the way to the small but functional galley kitchen. "There's a fresh loaf of bread on the counter if you don't mind slicing it. The knife is in the butcher block next to the sink."

"This wouldn't happen to be Belle's bread, would it?"

"Yes, it is. She's been on a bread-making kick ever since she got pregnant."

"Oh, my God, I love Belle's bread. She gave me a loaf a few weeks ago and I am not ashamed to admit I had intended to share it with my family, but I wound up eating half the loaf on the way to Missoula. It was so good, I didn't feel like sharing the rest with them, so I ate the other half on the way home."

"Should I make the whole pound of bacon, then?"

"Hey, now." She swatted him on the shoulder. "I don't eat that much. I mean I could, but I try not to. Unless it's something really good."

Garrett watched her remove the eggs from the refrigerator and set them on the counter. She opened the glass-front cabinet, grabbed a ceramic mixing bowl and began cracking eggs into it. She looked natural standing in his kitchen. And he found that comforting and scary at the same time.

"Garbage disposal or trash can?"

"I'm sorry, what?" Garrett stepped around her to get the bacon out of the freezer.

"Do you want the shells in the trash can or do you have a garbage disposal?"

"I have a disposal, but Belle composts everything and asks us to keep all scraps." He opened the fridge and removed a large covered coffee can and sat it on the counter next to her. "The shells go in there. I'll drop it off later when I pick up the kids."

"Your family is really close, isn't it?"

"Yes and no." Garrett unwrapped the bacon, set it on a plate and popped it in the microwave. "Harlan, Dylan and I are. After our other brother—Ryder—went to jail for running over and killing our father, the family kind of split in half." He stabbed the buttons on the front panel, causing the entire microwave to slide backwards and bang into the backsplash.

Delta gasped. "That's terrible."

"Supposedly it was an accident, but Ryder was drunk

and they were arguing." Garrett sighed. "I still don't know what to believe."

"I can't even fathom what that must be like for you and your family. What about your mom?"

"She moved out to California and remarried. My youngest brother, Wes, stayed on the road bull riding most of the time until he moved to Texas a few weeks ago. And Rebecca and I moved out to Wyoming."

"Were you happy there?"

Garrett ran his hands under the faucet and dried them, willing himself to talk about Rebecca without breaking down.

"We found out Rebecca had pancreatic cancer shortly after my father died."

"Oh, Garrett. I am so sorry." She lifted her hand to reach for him, then hesitated. This was the one time he wished she followed through.

"And then she was gone. I had two major deaths within two years. I didn't really know what to do or where I belonged, so that's when I moved in with my in-laws. And then here." Garret checked the remaining time on the microwave "What about you? Do you have a big family?"

"My mom, dad and my two brothers—Trevor and Cooper—live in Missoula. None of the kids are married and none of us have kids of our own. It's just the five of us."

"Earlier you said you had been married. Mind if I ask what happened?"

Delta stiffened at the question. "My husband cheated on me while I was battling cancer."

Garrett felt as if someone had kicked him in the gut

and then sucked all the air out of his body. "You had cancer?"

Delta randomly opened and closed drawers until she found a whisk and then began furiously beating the eggs. "I had stage IIIb Hodgkin's lymphoma."

He reached for her hands and stilled them. She turned toward him and looked up. Tears brimmed her eyes, threatening to spill at any moment. "Why didn't you tell me this earlier when I told you about Rebecca?"

"Because you needed someone to listen. And I didn't want you to think I was being selfish or trying to diminish what had happened to your wife by telling you I fought cancer, too."

"Honey, that's not selfish. Cancer is selfish. Hell, it's the greediest son of a bitch I've ever met. But telling me you had cancer is not selfish. How long ago?"

Delta stepped away from him and washed her hands in the sink. She sighed deeply before answering. "Three years ago."

Garrett felt his heart shudder. "The same time as Rebecca?"

"Please forgive me for not telling you sooner." Her voice cracked as she gripped the edge of the sink. "I just didn't think you would want to hear that I had survived when the person you love more than life itself had died."

"Oh, Delta." He grabbed her hands and held them. "Rebecca died so Bryce could live. We found out she had cancer when she was six weeks pregnant. The doctors gave her options. And she chose life—Bryce's life over her own."

Delta pulled away and covered her mouth with her hands. "She made the ultimate sacrifice."

"She did and there was nothing I could do about it. I begged—I begged her to terminate the pregnancy and start treatment immediately. She refused. Do you know how guilty I feel whenever I look at my son?"

"Oh no, no, no, no. You can't think that way. You're allowed to want your wife to live."

"If she had listened to me, he wouldn't be alive but she would." Garrett sniffled and wiped at his eyes. "It's a sickening feeling. She wouldn't allow me to make any decisions. Rebecca made her choice and I had to accept it and pray. But some prayers don't get answered."

"But mine did." Delta choked back a sob. "Rebecca's should have, too."

"Her prayers were answered. She gave birth to a healthy child that she got to love for sixteen months. By the time she gave birth and started chemo it was too late. The cancer had already spread too much. But that was her choice. Your choice was to fight to survive and that's exactly the way it should be. Please don't think for even one second that I would have wanted you two to trade places. I would never think that, Delta. Never."

"I'm so sorry this happened to you." The tears she had fought so hard to keep in check streamed down her cheeks. "I'm so sorry."

Garrett wrapped her in his arms and held her tight. "I'm sorry, too." He buried his face in her hair, and for the first time in years, he allowed himself to cry.

Chapter Eight

Delta ran into the Silver Bells stables a half hour late on Tuesday. She was scheduled to meet with Lydia Presley to review Lightning Bug's new scans. She had purposely scheduled the appointment for late afternoon so she could take care of customers and meet with various vendors about the guest ranch's Valentine's event first. She had only been helping Garrett a few days and she already wanted to strangle Cupid more than she had before Garrett had roped her into helping him.

"I am so sorry. I got tied up." Delta dumped her tote bag on the floor outside Lightning Bug's stall.

"No biggie. I'm just pulling the images up on the screen now." Lydia eyed the fabric swatches and bridal magazines spilling out of the top of Delta's bag. "Are you getting married?"

"Who, me? Oh, hell no. Never again."

Lydia almost dropped her iPad at the comment. "Then what's with the bridal stuff?"

"They're for Garrett."

Lydia tilted her head to get a better view of the top magazine's cover. "I don't think a gown that low cut will look good on him. He doesn't have the cleavage to pull it off."

"Very funny." Delta tried to push the magazines down farther in the bag, but it had already reached its maximum capacity. "We're working together on a Valentine's week event for the ranch. I'm sort of partially responsible for Dylan designating him as the event planner, so he asked me to help him."

"I bet he did." Lydia winked. "Isn't he single?"

"Not you, too."

"What?" Lydia feigned innocence. "You're single. He's single. You're planning a Valentine thing together. Does Cupid have to hit you over the head with his arrow?"

"Me and Cupid had a falling-out a long time ago. Besides, Garrett isn't ready to date, which is why I've taken on so much of the responsibility. He's having a hard time with this. It reminds him of his wife. Plus, I'm not looking. This event is for people who are already together."

"Maybe they should consider a singles weekend. I could see where that would generate some interest."

"Then be my guest to discuss it with Dylan and Emma. I'm up to my eyeballs in trying to find budget-friendly ways to decorate the guest lodge and rooms for the event. I spoke to some of my friends last night and they told me to pick up some bridal magazines for romantic inspiration. I've already spoken with a few places today."

"You can rent everything from tableware to bedding nowadays."

"I already found some place settings I think will

work. But I didn't realize you could rent bedding?" Garrett had given her a tour of the lodge and cabins the other day. While the guest ranch was meant to be rustic, the rooms definitely needed some freshening up. There wasn't enough time or money to replace any of the furniture, but bedding would make a huge difference.

"You can rent everything down to the pillowcases and guest towels." Lydia enlarged the first scan of Lightning Bug's hoof. "Everything looks good on this one." She loaded the next image and studied it. "A lot of resorts use rental services to avoid having on-site laundry facilities. Look up linen rental online and I'm sure you'll find a few places nearby. You may even want to call some of the ski resorts and ask who they use."

"You just gave me an idea." Delta tugged her phone out of her back pocket and typed in a quick note before returning her attention to the scans. "What do you think?"

"Your corrective shoeing is doing exactly what it's supposed to. The inflammation is down, his limp is gone. I'm really pleased with his progress."

"Great!" Delta loved her job. It was backbreaking work, but at the end of the day she made a difference in a horse's quality of life. Especially when it came to corrective shoeing. A lame horse could face death if not treated quickly and properly.

"Good afternoon, ladies." Garrett greeted them in the corridor as they exited the stall. "How is he doing?"

"By spring he should be ready to ride the trails again. We'll revisit it more then. Just keep in mind he'll never be able to work every day like he used to. Not at his age. And he shouldn't carry more than eighty pounds, but I think he'll be happy getting back out there with his friends."

"What about if we retire him and let him spend the rest of his days grazing on the ranch."

"You can do that, too. Just keep in mind this is an animal that's used to human contact. If you retire him, make sure he's still handled and touched on a daily basis. Without that interaction, he can begin to experience a form of depression, much the same way humans do when we remove physical contact from their lives."

"I will definitely make sure he is spoiled rotten." Garrett reached into the stall and rubbed the horse's muzzle. "He was one of my uncle's favorites. He would want him to be happy." He turned to Delta. "Speaking of happy, I have something that should make you the happiest woman on this ranch."

"You have something for me?" She heard Lydia giggle behind her. "You didn't have to do that."

"Yeah, I sort of did." Garrett held out his hand. "But, you have to close your eyes and I'll lead the way. I don't want you to see it until we're there."

His strong, firm grip encircled her palm. She fought the urge to entwine her fingers in his, knowing that wasn't the reason he was holding her hand. This was no different than ice skating. There was nothing romantic about it.

"What is it, what is it?" Delta bounced up and down.

"You're worse than my kids. The man told you to close your eyes," Lydia chided.

"Do you know what it is?" Delta asked her.

"No, now close your eyes," she ordered. "Take baby steps so you don't trip and break something."

"How far away is it?"

"Daddy, Daddy." Delta heard Kacey's footsteps run down the corridor. "Are you giving Delta her surprise now?"

"I sure am, sweetheart. Why don't you take her other hand and we'll guide her there together?"

A small hand slid into hers and held on tight.

She squeezed her eyes shut in anticipation as they led her around in what began to feel like circles. "Hey, what are you two up to?"

The sound of Lydia's giggling behind her confirmed what she thought. They *were* going around in circles. The stable corridor wasn't that long and they hadn't gone outside. They stopped and Garrett squeezed her hand.

"You can open your eyes now."

Delta blinked a few times to adjust to the bright overhead light. "Oh, my God!" Her hands flew to her mouth. There at the end of the stables stood a new Amish Belgian shoeing stall. The craftsmanship was exquisite. When she had mentioned the ranch getting a shoeing stall she had envisioned a very basic tubular metal enclosure, never anything this grand. She stepped onto the platform and ran her hand over the smooth white oak. She wouldn't have to hold the Belgians' hooves up any more or deal with them leaning on her while she tried to work. "This is the nicest stock I have ever seen. And the lighting?" Delta looked up at the ceiling. "I don't remember you ever having lights this bright in here."

"Those are new, too." Garrett lifted his chin proudly. "I wanted to make sure you had everything you needed to do your job comfortably."

"Maybe you should look into buying the white dress," Lydia whispered behind her.

Delta swatted her away. "This was very sweet of you, Garrett. You have no idea how much I appreciate it. Thank you." Women could keep their fancy jewelry and expensive shoes. A shoeing stall was the way to this farrier's heart.

A tinge of pink crept into Garrett's cheeks. "There's no need to thank me. I'm embarrassed we didn't have what you needed before now."

"It may not have bothered Henry, so he probably never mentioned it."

"I'm glad you did and I'm glad you're happy. It's the least I can do for all you have done for this ranch over the past year."

She knew Garrett's gift didn't have any romantic undertones, but it was by far the sweetest thing anyone had done for her in years.

His darling daughter had twisted Delta's arm into joining them for dinner. It wasn't that he minded, he just didn't want Kacey's enthusiasm to overwhelm her. Ever since Kacey had opened up to Delta about being bullied he had seen a big change in her personality. The private school had been rough at first, but she was beginning to adjust and had begun coming home from school happier. Her confidence and determination had markedly improved. Homework used to be a battle, but last night, she started working on it without any prodding from him. That had been a definite first.

School had never been easy for Kacey. She always had to work twice as hard to keep up with the other kids. Her teachers had thought it was due to a lack of focus and concentration, but Garrett knew there was more to it than that.

Kacey had just entered preschool when Rebecca got sick. She had designated herself Bryce's primary caretaker shortly after his birth. She'd been changing his diapers and feeding him before she was five years old. It was too much for a child to handle. He hadn't wanted her taking on that responsibility, but she fought him with everything she had.

Kacey had believed if she took care of Bryce, it would free up his time to take care of her mother and she could get better. Her determination broke his heart, because they knew months before Rebecca had died that she wouldn't survive. It wasn't until Belle and Emma came into the picture that she began to relinquish some of her mothering role. But he still found her in Bryce's room most mornings getting him up and dressed for preschool.

"Are you sure you're okay teaching her guitar?" Garrett asked as Delta helped him clear the table while Kacey showed Jake her and Bryce's bedrooms. "I don't want you to feel obligated, especially when my brother plays."

"I'm fine with it. I enjoy spending time with Kacey." Delta set the rest of the dishes in the sink. "But if you're uncomfortable with it, I can make an excuse to leave."

"I love the idea." Garrett turned on the faucet and squirted a few drops of detergent into the sink. "Kacey's never expressed interest in a hobby before you came along. I think you're a good influence on her. It's nice to see her be a kid instead of trying to be so strong for everyone else, including me. I haven't been the best parent. I wore my grief on my sleeve and Kacey paid the price."

Her fingers rested on his bare arm, radiating warmth straight to his heart. "I think you're doing a remarkable job."

"Thank you." He covered her hand with his own. "I love that you're getting close to Kacey. My daughter has done a complete one-eighty since you walked into her life. I can never repay you for that."

"I don't expect you to."

Her gentle smile drew him into the depths of her charms. "You're wonderful with children, so I have to ask…have you given any thought to having any of your own?"

Delta's shoulders sagged. "Chemo destroyed any chance I had of having children." Delta raised her hand to stop him before he spoke. "Please don't say you're sorry. There's nothing to be sorry about. I made peace with it years ago. There are enough children out there in need of a good home that it makes me okay with not being able to have one biologically. I want kids and I'm prepared to do that without a partner. I just wish I didn't have to wait."

Garrett couldn't fathom being told he'd never be able to have a child of his own. The joy that came from the realization you helped create another living being was like no other. But he could also see himself loving a child that wasn't biologically his, as well.

"Why do you have to wait?"

"Adoption agencies won't consider my application until I'm cancer free for five years. And I get that. In the meantime, spending time with your kids helps fill that void. They really are wonderful children."

"But what if you got involved with someone who already has children?" Garrett froze as soon as he said the words. He hadn't meant to imply himself and he knew that was probably how it had sounded. Not that there was anything wrong with the idea, he just wasn't in the market for a wife. "I just mean there are plenty of single dads out there."

"Oh okay, because for a second there I thought you were—"

"Yeah, sorry, no. I—I don't think I'll ever be ready for that. Not with you."

"What?"

Oh crap! "I meant I'm not saying I'll never be ready for that with you. I'm trying to say I don't think I'll ever be ready, period."

"That makes me feel a little better." She started to laugh. "God, could you imagine?"

"What? Us?" Garrett pulled the drain stopper from the bottom of the sink. "I don't think there would ever be a dull moment."

Delta smiled and nodded. "That's for sure. You don't ever think about it? I don't mean us, I mean like ever with anyone?"

Garrett checked to make sure the kids hadn't wandered into the kitchen. "Rebecca told me to move on, so yeah, I do sometimes. But I don't know how to do that without feeling guilty. And maybe I'll get there someday, but I don't see it."

"You've got this, Garrett." Delta wrapped an arm around his shoulder and squeezed. "Give yourself time."

Garrett slid an arm around her waist, tugging her into a hug. "Thank you. That means a lot to me." He buried his head in her hair and held on. He hated to admit it, but he needed her strength to lean on tonight. The closer it was to the anniversary of Rebecca's death, the more he felt the need to let some of his grief go. After almost three years of keeping it inside, he needed... wanted the release.

"Can we have dessert now?" Kacey asked from the kitchen doorway as Bryce barreled past her and wrapped his arms around him and Delta, making it next to impossible for them to completely break their embrace.

"What about you, little man?" Garrett lifted Bryce into his arms, creating a makeshift barrier between himself and Delta. If Kacey had been bothered by their hug, she didn't show it. That was almost more concerning than if she had said something. He already knew how capable she was at hiding things from him. "Would you like some dessert?"

"Can I have cookies?" his son asked.

"We don't have cookies. Aunt Emma sent you home with brownies. You like brownies, don't you?"

"I thought she wasn't our aunt until she married Uncle Dylan."

Garrett shifted Bryce onto his other hip and smiled at Delta. "They're getting married in June, sweetheart. They have a baby and it's close enough."

He was already dreading the day his daughter asked him where babies came from. And considering her ever-growing attachment to Holly, he had a feeling it would come sooner than later.

He and Rebecca had expected her to ask when Bryce was born, but her mind had been more on her mother's illness than wondering how her baby brother came to be. A part of him hoped the school would beat him to it. But that was the easy way out and his daughter deserved to hear it from him first, regardless of how difficult the conversation would be.

Good Lord. The thought of that alone made him cringe. He still felt like they were learning how to communicate with one another without Terry and Dawn. He'd never had to explain anything when they'd lived in Wheatland. It was all done for him. And that was just as much his fault if not more than it was his in-laws'. He still loved them dearly, but he had given them way too much control. While he was grieving, they had kept his life very neat and tidy. Now it was anything but. And in a way, he liked that better. He was slowly learning that sometimes you had to shake things up to make them better.

Garrett lowered Bryce to the floor. "Daddy's going to finish cleaning up the kitchen and then we'll have dessert."

"Can Delta start teaching me guitar while we wait?"

"That's a great idea." Garrett smiled at his daughter. "You keep her busy in there so she won't forget she's a guest in our home because she doesn't need to clean up after us."

It would give him some much-needed distance away from her. Twice now, he'd found himself hugging his farrier in the kitchen. All right, his friend the farrier. Either way, it was beginning to feel familiar. He wanted to fight against it. He didn't want to feel anything other than friendship toward Delta, but the more time he spent around her, the more he looked forward to the next time. Hell, as they were eating dinner tonight he'd caught himself thinking about what he would cook the next time she came over. He had no right to assume she even wanted to come back. Although, she did seem to enjoy their time together as much as they enjoyed having her.

"Okay, okay. Message received," she said to Garrett. "Let me grab my guitar from the Jeep and take Jake out for a potty break and then we'll start your lesson."

"Can I come with you?" Kacey asked.

"Me, too!" Bryce ran into the living room.

"Stay inside, you two. It's too cold to go out without jackets and I don't have the energy to bundle the two of you up right now. Delta is only going outside for a minute. Unless you plan on making a break for it." He winked and instantly regretted it. He was flirting and he had no right to.

"You're not going to get rid of me that easily." She winked in return. Okay, they were both flirting and maybe he didn't regret it so much after all.

FOR THE NEXT hour, he and Bryce colored at the table while Delta taught his daughter guitar in the living room. Kacey's million and one questions were enough to try anyone's patience, but Delta's laughter dispelled any concerns he might have. He peeked in at them a few times, and was surprised to see Kacey laser focused on the instrument. He had never seen her that interested in anything. Ever. He'd give it a few more lessons before he asked Delta to help him pick out a guitar for her birthday. More and more, he liked the idea of an instrument over a puppy. One adjustment at a time.

They were finally beginning to settle into somewhat of a normal routine in Saddle Ridge. Emma had volunteered to pick Kacey up from school every day, since the private school didn't provide bus service like the public school had. She had already been watching Bryce after preschool, now she had taken on his daughter.

The arrangement was fine for now, but he needed to find a more permanent solution. Emma would eventually be working full-time at the lodge and she would have her hands full between that and her own child. He felt as if he was taking advantage, but she said Kacey was a big help to her with Holly.

The past few days had given him hope. Hope they would survive as a family. There had been times after the move when he'd wondered if his kids would have preferred if he'd walked away and left them with their grandparents. In the back of his mind, he wondered if that had been Dawn and Terry's master plan.

When he had taken over as their ranch manager, he quickly began to lose touch with his children. He didn't bond with Bryce until he was almost a year old. Before that, in all the grief and depression, Bryce was just a baby he was responsible for. But when the fog lifted, it was as if somebody had flicked a switch. That was when he'd decided to take back control of his children. Garrett needed his kids, and his in-laws didn't want to alienate him for fear he would leave with the children. Which ultimately was what happened—not because he was angry or felt threatened. But because it was time.

"Daddy!" Kacey ran into the kitchen with an ear-to-ear smile. "Did you hear me play?"

"Yes, I did. You sounded great, sweetheart."

"My fingers are sore from pushing the strings down on the frets but Delta said I'll grow calloused after a while."

"You'll form calluses," Delta gently corrected. "Let's hope you never grow calloused."

"And Delta said she will loan me one of her guitars to play on since I don't have one."

"That's awfully generous, Delta, but are you sure you want to take that risk?" He feared his daughter would damage the hollow body of an acoustic guitar. "Maybe you should take a few more lessons first."

"I have an older travel guitar at the house that will fit her perfectly. I don't use it that much anymore. I take my parlor guitar back and forth to the convalescent home since it's smaller than the one I normally play." She smiled up at him. "It will give her something to practice on until she decides if this is what she really wants."

"Thank you." Her generosity with his kids continued to amaze him. He'd be lying if he said he didn't sometimes wonder what life would be like having her around more often. "Now, who wants brownies and ice cream?"

"I do, I do!" Bryce climbed on top of his chair.

"Be careful, peanut." Before he could even react, Delta reached over the back of the chair, lifted Bryce up and reseated him. "You don't want to fall and get hurt."

With every minute that passed, every movement she made, Garrett saw her fall in step with their lives. And while the timing was wrong, maybe someday there would be a chance of more.

"I found out not only can we rent linens and place settings, we can rent red, pink and white aprons." Delta poured coffee for her and Dylan while he unwrapped the platter of brownies and sat it on the center of the table. "But we need to get our order in right away because some of the Western designs aren't in stock locally. They'll need a few days to ship them in. I brought the catalog and swatches with me."

Garrett blew out a breath. "Great, thank you." He still hadn't forgiven Dylan for dumping Valentine's Day on him especially when it was so close to the anniversary of Rebecca's death. He'd taken notice of how careful Delta had been to keep their plans simple and tasteful. "When I wrangled you into this, I hadn't expected you to do so much. You've gone above and beyond."

"You have your hands full with kids and work."

"You have a pretty packed schedule yourself."

"Yeah, but my four-legged child is easier to take care of."

"I want a doggie!" Bryce shouted across the table.

"Yeah, Daddy, when can we get a dog?"

Delta looked at him and started laughing. "Looks like your hands are going to be fuller than I thought." She ruffled Bryce's hair. "How about I loan you Jake from time to time. Would that make you happy?"

"Yay!" The kids cheered from their chairs.

Good save, Garrett mouthed to her.

"I'll add it to your tab." Delta set the cups on the table and grabbed a stack of napkins from the drawer near the fridge. "I also found out there's a hospitality service in Kalispell that will come in daily and handle the laundry service. I'm thinking white. Luxurious white Egyptian cotton sheets, white fluffy towels and bathrobes, and white bedding. I think the higher-end bedding will contrast the rustic wood in the rooms and cabins, giving it a Western flair without being in-your-face obvious."

"I wouldn't have chosen white, but I can picture that." A flash of the two of them sharing one of those rooms played in his mind. He shook his head to clear the thought. "Sounds great."

"I printed out some amazing menus from similar guest ranches in California. Maybe we could elevate the menu just a little bit for this event." Delta crossed the room and picked up the overstuffed tote bag she had left against the wall when she'd come in. She rummaged through it before removing a thick folder. "This should be a great start for you and the staff." She traded him the folder for a gallon of milk and two glasses for the kids. "Maybe pick one thing from each menu and create your own? The chefs may even want to add their spin on it. How about asking them to create a special Valentine's Day menu and just use these as ideas. Delegate it to them. They're the chefs."

He watched her lovingly tuck a napkin into Bryce's third shirt of the day and set a small piece of brownie in front of him before opening the ice cream. "Don't worry, peanut, there's more where that came from." Why was it the women in his life knew to feed Bryce in small increments yet he and his in-laws had struggled with getting him to eat like a child should?

"Red roses are at a ridiculous premium." She spooned out a scoop of ice cream in each of the kids' bowls before putting the carton away. "A friend of mine suggested white roses. They're a little more elegant, will go perfectly with the white theme and will look beautiful against red table linens. Oh, I know!" She jumped up and dove into her bag again. "There is a warm red plaid linen I saw in a catalog. Think flannel shirt. White rose centerpieces would look stunning on them." She thumbed through the catalog before finding the page, and handed it to him. "This one. And I had three florists send me centerpiece ideas along with pricing. Two of them said they could provide long-stem roses every evening for turndown service. That would be a nice touch to add to a bed on top of your standard chocolate."

Once again, he envisioned sharing a room with Delta, only it wasn't at a hotel. It was at home. Their home. A home he'd never been to but one where she fluttered around the kitchen tending to his children as she was now. A home free of pain and filled with his children's laughter. A home with a master bedroom and a door they could tuck themselves behind at night.

"Daddy." Kacey tugged on his arm. "Delta's talking to you."

"What, oh, we don't have turndown service." Garrett pulled out a chair and flopped down on it. He didn't understand what was happening. He wasn't ready to daydream of a future with Delta. It was still too soon.

"Well, you will for Valentine's week. Figure two staff members can quickly run around and do it while your guests are dining." Delta pulled Bryce's ice-cream-covered fingers out of the bowl and wiped them off. "That's not a finger food." She gently wrapped his hand around a spoon and guided him to the bowl. "Hold it like this and take a small spoonful." She returned her attention to Garrett. "What have you found by way of entertainment?"

Garrett forced his brain to focus on the Valentine's retreat and not the loving and helpful way she attended to his kids. "Um, most of the people I contacted were already booked that week. I think anything structured will detract from Silver Bells' ambience, if we can call it that at this stage. People who come here don't expect to be serenaded while they're eating."

"So you have nothing?" she questioned.

"I just thought we could take it in a different direction. Dylan does sing-alongs in front of our big stone fireplace and I wouldn't mind adding something similar outside around our fire pit in the back. We serve hot chocolate out there at night and the guests make s'mores. A guitarist out there would be nice, too."

"I saw something online the other day about elevated s'mores." Delta's face brightened with each idea. "Some had bacon, others had strawberries. Maybe the staff could make some sort of fancier base to replace the Graham crackers. Maybe a cookie or even a pastry."

"You have good ideas, Delta." Kacey's chair was inches from hers and Garrett couldn't help but smile at the way his daughter hung on her every word.

"Thank you, sweetie." Delta gave her a quick hug. "I wish I could take credit for all of them, but my girlfriends had a lot of ideas from when they planned their weddings."

"Do you want to get married?" Kacey asked.

"Uh." Her eyes widened. "I'm not dating anyone, so I can't get married."

Good save, Delta. He picked up his mug of coffee and took a sip.

"I thought you were dating Daddy."

Garrett began to choke.

"Are you all right?" Delta smacked him on the back. "Put your arms over your head." She grabbed his hands and raised them in the air before he had a chance to comply.

He continued to cough for another minute before waggling his finger at Kacey. "Delta and I are just friends."

"But you bought her that gift."

"That wasn't a gift," Delta corrected. "The shoeing stall is for work."

"And you were hugging before."

"Sometimes friends hug." Garrett scrubbed his jaw. "Honey, I'm not dating anyone. Delta and I work together and we're good friends, but that's all." He didn't blame his daughter for being confused. Between dinner at Harlan's and everything else Kacey had witnessed, even Garrett had a bit of trouble distinguishing what was and what wasn't where Delta was concerned. She fit comfortably in their lives and that reality was easily blurred while she was there. "Do you understand?"

"I guess." Kacey climbed off her chair and took her half-eaten bowl of ice cream to the sink. "Can I go try some of the notes you taught me on guitar?"

"Go right ahead." Delta's bittersweet smile helped ease the tension, but they both knew they had to be more careful.

"I've added more excursion choices to our standard winter selection." Garrett attempted to redirect the conversation back to work. "There's a dogsledding company not far from here that specializes in couples' sledding. They give lessons and send them on a romantic one-hour adventure. They gave me two dates we can book during that week."

"I'm so jealous." Delta sighed. "I have always wanted to go dogsledding."

"We should go sometime." And there went any chance of him focusing on work for the rest of the night.

Their relationship had changed without him realizing it. Ever since Delta had told him she was a cancer survivor he looked at her differently. There was a delicate vulnerability along with her strength. And that combination had awoken a part of him he thought had died with Rebecca. His heart had stirred and it had begun to beat a little brighter...for her. For a future. And that terrified him.

Chapter Nine

The following day, Delta still couldn't get Kacey's comment about her and Garrett dating out of her head. She had to admit, it had begun to feel that way. And as much as she said she would never date a client, Garrett had slowly become the one exception. In her mind only. The man wasn't ready to date and who knew if he ever would be. But damned if the idea wasn't growing on her.

The morning had been relatively quiet, which she'd been thankful for. Even though she'd slept well, she was still tired. Ever since Garrett came into her life, her entire body was out of whack...beginning with her brain, which needed to be examined for even thinking about any attraction to the man.

Those kids, though...they did something to her every time she was around them. When she had offered to teach Kacey guitar, she never expected to get attached to her or her brother. But every morning since then, she'd awoken with them on her mind...along with Garrett.

He had asked her if she had ever thought about dating a man with kids, and honestly, it hadn't crossed her mind before. She'd always thought of her parenting future as a solo venture. But now...yeah, she could. She'd fallen for Bryce's cute-as-a-button charm and his melt-your-heart smile that rivaled his father's. And Kacey reminded Delta so much of herself at that age. Same love of music. Same curiosity.

On her drive home last night, she couldn't wait to see them again. She wanted to be a part of their lives and watch them grow into adults. And that was something she had no right to want. They weren't her children.

It was shortly after eleven when she left the convalescent home with Jake. She climbed in her work truck and removed her cell phone from the charger. One missed call. Garrett. She tried to ignore the double-time beat of her heart when she listened to his voice mail.

"Hi, Delta, it's Garrett. My head chef suggested we have a bakery cater some specialty pastries during Valentine's week. I have an appointment with Tiers of Joy Confectioners on Central Avenue today at twelve thirty. I don't know if you're free or take a lunch break around then, but I'd love to get your input."

The thought of tasting pastry with Garrett made her giddy. Delta wasn't a giddy girl. She should say no. But who can pass up pastry?

"How would you like to spend the afternoon at Bow-WowWowzer's?" Jake barked in recognition of the name. Delta had just enough time to drop him off at doggie daycare and change into more appropriate pastry eating attire.

She dialed Garrett's number and waited for him to answer. Instead, she got his voice mail.

"Hi, it's Delta. I'd love to meet you at twelve thirty. See you then."

Love? Why did she use that word? It was too late to do anything about it now.

An hour later, Delta parked her Jeep in front of the bakery. She scanned the street for Garrett's SUV but didn't see it. She didn't want to go in without him, although it was ridiculous not to. They might even give her an extra sample if she did. Instead, she chose to sit in her car and wait, her hands still on the steering wheel, sweating.

Why was she nervous? She was going to have her cake and eat it, too. Who didn't like that? The last time she went to a bakery for a tasting was before her wedding. Eddie had crept into her thoughts far too many times over the past couple weeks. She had successfully kept his memory at bay until Garrett appeared. The man invoked far too many feels for her to want to deal with. Yet, here she was, waiting for him.

And there he was, walking down the sidewalk toward her. She ran her palms up and down her jeans, cursing herself for not bringing her gloves. He opened the door as she reached for the handle. The perfect gentleman as always.

"Thank you for doing this with me," he said as she stepped onto the pavement. "I don't know a napoleon from cannoli. Well, I do, but—oh, you know what I mean."

Delta tried not to laugh. He was as nervous as she was and it was just dessert. They were going to eat sugar and be happy. She looked up at him, waiting for him to move. But he stood there, staring down at her.

"Um, is something wrong?" Delta examined her clothes. She'd chosen a pair of jeans and a fitted purple pullover. It wasn't fancy, but it wasn't too casual either. Nope, nothing was exposed.

"I, uh." He buried his hands in his coat pockets, only it wasn't the barn jacket he normally wore. Instead, he had on a double-breasted navy wool peacoat and it fit him beautifully. Too beautifully. She never would've chosen that cut for him, but whoever had knew what they were doing. "Never mind." He turned away and walked to the door of the bakery.

Now it was her turn not to move. Was she missing something?

"It was nothing," he said as if reading her thoughts. "I was going to ask you something. But it can wait."

Delta hated when people did that. Now she would wonder what he wanted to ask until he actually asked it.

"Hi, I'm Joy Lancaster, you must be Garrett. It's a pleasure to meet you." The woman wasn't at all what Delta had expected. She had pictured a middle-aged baker in a chef's coat, not a twentysomething stunner dressed in a black fitted flare skirt and a white short-sleeve blouse, with platinum-blond hair in glamorous '40s retro victory rolls.

"Same here. And this is Delta Grace, she's helping me decide what we'll need."

"Great. If you follow me, I have twenty different pastries for you to try in our tasting room."

Garrett looked at Delta and mouthed, *Oh my God, twenty?* Even Delta wasn't sure she could sample twenty pastries, but she was going to have fun trying. Either that or she'd explode.

They entered a small chicly decorated room located next to the kitchen. The walls were a creamy white, but the ceiling and floor were black, which gave the room a floating appearance. A white bistro table and chairs with black trim was elegantly set with fine china and real silverware. Suddenly Delta felt underdressed.

"Here, let me take your coats," Joy offered.

Garrett held out her chair, as she eyed the delectable display waiting for them.

"Let's begin with a simple macaron." Joy sat a colorful plate of delicate cookies before them. And they were anything but simple. "The lavender one is crème brûlée flavored, the orange is passion fruit with a dark chocolate center, the green is fresh mint with white chocolate and the gray is black currant."

Delta carefully sliced each macaron in half so they could each taste one. And they were exquisitely rich yet airy and light on the tongue.

"I'm already at a loss for words," Garrett said.

All Delta could do was nod. Words couldn't describe how ethereal they tasted.

"Our next selection is a cream horn." Joy set a puffed pastry covered in powdered sugar between them. "This is made with one of our flakiest pastries and is filled with apricot jam and whipped cream. We shape the horn by winding overlapping pastry strips around a cone-shaped mold."

Garrett served half the horn to Delta before sampling his half. "I don't think I've ever had dessert melt in my mouth before."

"I second that."

After tasting an éclair, palmier, galette and a slice of Linzer torte, Delta thought she had died and gone to heaven. She also didn't think she could eat another bite. Three shared slices of cake, two tarts, strudel and a chocolate profiterole later, Delta could no longer move or form sentences. She had officially reached her limit.

"Delta, you have to try this." Garrett inched his chair closer to hers as he held up a bite-size piece of Paris-Brest. The buttery choux pastry and praline-flavored cream beckoned her to open her mouth as he fed her the delicacy. The intimacy of the gesture sent her thoughts in a much different direction. She didn't know if it was the seduction of the French pastry or his closeness, but suddenly she wanted more of both.

"That's sinful and in more than one way."

"It sure is." Garrett ran his thumb over her bottom lip. "You had a little something."

She wanted more than a little something. The man was making her feel warm in places that didn't need to feel warm. At least not right now. She ached to remove her clothes and quell her increasing desire for the one man she couldn't have.

CHECK PLEASE! If only it were that simple. Garrett's arousal took him off guard. He was human, so an erection wasn't an unusual thing. But the desire to make love to Delta definitely was. After Rebecca, he had thought that part of his life was over. Meeting Delta had changed all that. Ever since Kacey had announced she thought he and Delta were dating, he'd started to see the potential of a future with another woman. Not just any woman. One woman. And while guilt and fear continued to creep into those thoughts, the fear of never knowing what could have been began to take control. Delta wasn't going anywhere and there was no rush, but waiting to see where their relationship went bordered on agonizing. He had already convinced her to be friends and she had unknowingly convinced him to give love a second chance, but he didn't know where to begin.

He had never really asked anyone out on a date. He and Rebecca had just happened. They had gone to school together, they had hung out together and before long, they had been boyfriend and girlfriend. He couldn't remember ever asking her to be with him. They had been a given. Dating was a foreign concept. He wanted to ask Delta out, but he didn't know how or if she would accept.

After choosing six different pastries to serve to the ranch's guests for Valentine's week, they left the bakery with one hunger sated.

Delta stopped short in front of him. "Okay, ask me."

He sidestepped her to keep from running into her. "Ask you what?"

"Whatever it was you were going to ask me before we went into Tiers of Joy. You said you would tell me later. Now is later."

"You really know how to put a guy on the spot, don't you?"

She gave him an impatient shrug. "You're stalling."

"I dreaded this tasting all day." A wave of mixed emotions surged through him. "I was afraid it would remind me of the cake tasting Rebecca and I had gone to before our wedding."

"I had the same fear. I immediately thought of my cake tasting, too. But it was different."

"Exactly." Garrett leaned against the side of her Jeep.

"It was fun and I don't think I would have enjoyed it with anyone other than you."

"I feel the same way."

"The more time I spend around you, the more chances I want to take in life."

"Okay." She folded her arms across her chest and stared at him.

Why was this so difficult? "Life is short."

"Yes, it is." She closed the distance between them and entwined her fingers in his. "It's okay to talk about her if that's what you want."

"That's not what I want." Garrett placed her hands on his chest and covered them. He looked skyward and prayed Rebecca wouldn't hate him for what he was about to do. "Um, I have never asked a woman out before."

There. He'd said it. It was out in the open.

"Oh." Her body stiffened.

Oh? That's all she had. She could have at least let him know if she was open to the idea.

Delta drew in a breath and released it before speaking. "Well?"

"Well what?" His mind whirled at her curt question.

"You can't just drop a bomb on someone like that. I get that you've never asked someone out based on what you've told me about you and Rebecca. But you haven't told me who you want to ask out."

Either Delta was blind or he was horrible at asking a woman on a date. "Delta." He gently squeezed her hands. "I'm asking you…will you go out with me?"

She let out a soft sigh of relief. "For a second there

I thought you were going to ask me to help you ask someone else out."

"No, Delta. There's no one else but you." He stared at her in disbelief.

"Are you sure you're ready to date again?" Delta bit her bottom lip before looking away.

He hooked her chin with his finger and angled her face toward his. "Only if it's with you. I'm tired of this permanent sorrow weighing me down. I want to feel alive again, Delta. And I want to feel it with you."

She regarded him carefully, making him even more nervous. "But you've been extremely closed off to the idea, so please understand my hesitation."

"Last night was an eye-opener. My daughter had automatically assumed we were together and she was all right with it. When I saw you with my kids and in my house, everything clicked. It felt right. For the first time in three years, I felt good and that was because I was there with you and the kids. We were this complete package and after you left last night, I missed you."

"And the guilt?" Her voice softened.

"I'm not going to lie and say it's not there, but it's not as strong as I thought it would be. I'm beginning to see things differently. I know you have a rule about not dating customers and I'm not asking you to make any commitment past one date."

"What if it doesn't work out?" Concern etched across her face.

"Then we go back to being friends. It won't change our business relationship. I'd like to think I'm mature enough to separate that from my personal life. I would hope you'd do the same."

"What did you have in mind?"

"Oh, no you don't." Garrett shook his head. "You're not getting any details until you give me an answer. This is the last time I'm asking... Delta Grace, will you go out with me?"

Heat visibly rose to her cheeks. "Yes, I will."

"Then let me take you horseback riding this afternoon, before the ranch opens for business tomorrow. There's something special about riding when no one else is around. I know it's still chilly out, but it's warmer than it's been all week." He smiled gently. "And if we're both still comfortable with the idea afterwards, maybe we can get a drink. I'd offer you dinner but I'm not sure either one of us will be hungry tonight after eating pastries for the last hour." Delta laughed at that. "Think of it as baby steps for both of us. You're uncertain about bending your rules and I'm uncertain about opening my heart."

The more Garrett tried to convince her to say yes, the more things he wanted to share with her. Not just around the ranch. Parts of his life and his family. And for the first time, he was thinking about removing his wedding ring.

"Don't you have to work, especially with the ranch reopening tomorrow?"

"I'm the boss. They can do without me for a few hours, plus if there's an emergency I'll have my phone on me."

"I'd love to." Delta stood on her toes and kissed him softly on the cheek. And somehow that one sweet kiss meant more to him than any make-out session ever would. There was hope, happiness and the chance of a future all rolled in that one tender gesture. And already his heart felt fuller than it had in years. He could only imagine what their next kiss would bring.

Chapter Ten

Delta's hands shook as she followed Garrett back to Silver Bells. Why was she so nervous? It wasn't like they had never been alone together. It just hadn't been anything beyond friendship. A date meant there was a kiss or something more intimate to come. Although Delta had always considered kissing quite intimate. And while she had initiated the peck on the cheek, she couldn't help but wonder what a full-on kiss would feel like. It wasn't the first time she'd wondered that either.

She giggled, filling the interior of her Jeep with girlish laughter. Garrett made her feel more feminine than any man ever had. And that included Eddie. Garrett had an innocent soul. His heart may be jaded, as was hers, but there was a raw pureness about him she'd never experienced before.

"Welcome to our first date," Garrett said later as he led her through the stables to Lucy's and Desi's stalls.

"We're riding the Belgians?" She squelched a tiny shriek of joy. When Garrett asked Delta to go riding with him on the ranch, she'd never expected to ride one of the Belgians. She had admired the breed her entire life, but hadn't had the opportunity to sit astride the magnificent animal. She knew their strength firsthand from working on them, but riding would be an entirely new experience.

She waited eagerly as Garrett saddled the horses. Weighing in at a ton each, they were almost double the weight of her quarter horses back in Missoula and eight inches taller.

"Would you like a leg up?" Garrett offered his hand and she appreciated the boost into the saddle. After eating all those pastries, she didn't think she'd manage to mount without it.

They rode silently across Silver Bells, until they reached the far edge of the property, a ridge overlooking the entire town. "It's stunning here." Delta reined her horse alongside Garrett. "I didn't realize the ranch had this kind of view. And there's my house!" She pointed in the distance. Although it looked more like a dot compared to the newer and larger homes being built on the land behind it.

"Come with me," Garrett said as he eased down from his saddle. He took her hand and led her over the hard-packed snow. "Once the ground thaws, we'll start building a gazebo here. Dylan designed it as a wedding present for Emma. They'll be the first of many to recite their vows and begin their lives together on this very spot."

"What a beautiful place for a wedding." Delta spun around, taking in the Swan Range and Mission Mountains off in the distance. As the sun began to dip lower in the Montana sky, she snaked both of her arms around Garrett's arm and gave it a squeeze. "Despite what you said the other day, you really are a romantic."

"I like to think I still have a few tricks up my sleeve." Garrett slid his arm out from under hers and wrapped it around her shoulders. "See, taking a ride with me wasn't so bad."

"I didn't think it would be bad, I just had to be sure this is what you wanted."

"What do you want, Delta?" His deep voice whispered against her ear, sending a delightful shiver down her spine.

She lifted her eyes to his. She had a fervent need to kiss him. To feel his mouth upon hers, but she refused to make the first move for fear he wasn't ready. The back of his fingers lightly grazed her cheek as her heart thudded in excitement, his gaze equally as soft as his caress. Her fingers ached to touch him, to hold him closer and explore what lay beneath the warm flannel of his shirt.

"You've affected me in a way I never thought possible." He lightly swept the hair away from her neck and kissed it ever so gently. Just one kiss that left her longing for more. "Is it okay that I touch you?"

"Yes." His nearness gave her comfort and made her body ache with desire at the same time.

"Is it okay if I kiss you?" His breath was hot against her cheek.

"Please," she whispered as his mouth covered hers. His lips gently caressed hers, sending spirals of desire coursing through her veins. "Garrett." Delta's voice was barely audible above her ragged breathing. "I've never been kissed like that before."

"You deserve to be kissed thoroughly every day, all day." He sighed and rested his forehead against hers. "I don't know where this will lead, but I want to find out. Are you willing to take a chance with me?"

"Yes, are you?"

"Yes." Garrett shifted, allowing the length of her body to press against his. His desire was evident both in his eyes and physically. "I want this, Delta. I want you."

She knocked his hat to the ground and buried her hands in his hair, fighting every urge to wrap her legs around his waist. She'd felt passion before, but nowhere near this intense. And never this strong. He enveloped her in strength, melting any resolve she once had.

He unzipped her jacket and slid his hands beneath her shirt, exploring the hollows of her back before settling on her waist. She yearned for them to caress every inch of her body. She arched against him, silently begging.

"I want you," he whispered against her mouth. "I want to make love to you until the sun comes up."

And she wanted him, too. She wanted to feel the length of him inside her. She wanted him to touch the very core of her soul. And as much as she didn't want to stop, she knew it was too soon. For both of them.

"Garrett, we can't. Not yet." His wounded gaze implored hers for an explanation. "When you make love to me, I want you to be a hundred percent certain. I want us both to be. Twenty-four hours ago, we both said this was impossible. I don't want to rush anything. And I don't want to ruin anything."

"Oh, I definitely plan on taking my time with you."

Delta's knees began to weaken. One arm wrapped around her for support while his fingers continued to explore under her clothes. They seared against her flesh despite the cool air around them. As he reached the band of her bra, he searched for a clasp, pleased when he found one in the front. With a flick of his thumb, he freed her breasts. Her breath caught in her throat as he lifted her shirt, exposing her to him. The Montana breeze hovered just above freezing as it danced across her nipples, hardening them further. His rough hands claimed her breasts, covering them completely with his palms. Sliding her sweater up, he bent forward and allowed his tongue to caress them, slowly taking each one into his mouth as he teased her to the very edge of desire.

"Garrett, if you keep this up, you're going to make me—"

"I know." He returned his attention to her mouth, his lips more persuasive as his tongue parted her lips. His fingers trailed down her abdomen, seeking the button of her jeans. She knew she should stop him, but she was powerless against the anticipation. He slowly eased her zipper down. Breaking their kiss, his eyes met hers as his fingers slid between her folds. He watched her as she rode the first wave of release, exciting her further. His rhythm powerful and firm, he sent her over the edge a second time, as his eyes raked every exposed inch of her body. She felt electrified, giving herself to him so freely out in the open. "And that's just the beginning of what's to come once I do make love to you. And we will make love, Delta."

"ARE YOU SURE you can't stay for dinner?" Garrett asked as he unsaddled Lucy and Desi. "Dylan and Emma would love to have you join us."

"Thanks for the invite, but I need to pick up Jake and stop by my friend Liv's house." Delta slid the saddle blankets off the Belgians' backs and followed Garrett into the tack room. "She's expecting triplets and is having a difficult time with her pregnancy."

"Liv Scott?"

"Yes, you know her?"

"I know her and her sister Jade. Wes is good friends with Liv." He removed two polar fleece coolers from the wall and started to laugh. "He moved to Texas shortly after she announced her pregnancy. You don't think?"

"Good heavens, no." Delta grabbed a hoof pick and a curry comb from the shelf and walked back to the horses. "Liv used an anonymous sperm and egg donor. Your brother's off the hook."

"I'm relieved, but in a way, I wish we had triplets running around the ranch." Garrett draped Lucy in a cooler-coat to help wick the moisture away from her skin. "Babies liven up a place. Oh, Delta. I'm sorry. I completely forgot."

"No, it's fine. I'm fine." She began brushing the snow from both horses' legs. "Liv was in a similar position. She couldn't conceive either. Through donors, she found a way to have the children and the family she wanted without a husband or complications, for the most part. She's in the middle of her second trimester and despite the all-day nausea, she and the babies are healthy." Delta attempted to lift one of Lucy's front hooves. "Come on girl, we've been working on this for a year. Lift for me." Reluctantly the horse obliged so Delta could clean the snow out of her winter shoes, and Garrett noticed how much she leaned on her, reconfirming he'd made the right decision purchasing the Amish shoeing stall. "In two years, it will be my turn."

"Could you carry if you wanted to?" Garrett winced at his own question. "I'm sorry, that was way too personal."

"It's all right." She cleared the snow from the center of the snow pad sandwiched between the snow-tire-like shoe and the animal's hoof. "I have the same options as Liv. I can carry a donor embryo, but I've chosen not to. Plus, I can't afford it and my insurance doesn't cover it. Maybe if I was married and my husband wanted a child, then I would consider it, but it's difficult being a pregnant farrier. I know one woman who shod up until the day she delivered, but she had an apprentice handling her rasping and shaping. It's not the safest job, especially when you're dealing with the hind legs. Plus, the downtime after delivery. And that's even longer when you have a cesarean." She moved on to Desi's hooves. "If it hadn't been for the cancer and my divorce, I probably would've continued to work for my father until I had a family, then I would've branched out on my own. But life's not perfect and when I examined my available options, I decided on adoption. Now it's a waiting game. I'll get my turn. I'll have my kids."

"Hopefully you'll have someone special by your side so you don't have to raise a child alone," he said after the horses were in their stalls. "It's not easy being a single parent."

"If I find the right person, then I would love to raise a family with them."

"How will you know it's the right person?"

She regarded him for a moment before answering.

"How does anyone know they're with the right person? I thought I had married the right person. Maybe if the circumstances had been different, we would still be together, but we're not. I don't think you ever truly know. At some point, you just have to have faith."

Garrett walked her outside, not wanting to say good-bye. He wanted to know more about her and her life before Saddle Ridge. "I wish you could stay, but a pregnant friend with triplets comes before a cowboy any day. Tell Liv I said hello."

"I will, and thanks for the ride. I really enjoyed it."

"It was my pleasure." Garrett tried not to laugh at his ironic choice of words.

"No, I think it was mine. But thanks for that, too." She winked and opened the Jeep's door.

"Not so fast." Garrett braced an arm on either side of her head. "I want one more for the road." He pressed his lips gently against hers. The touch alone was a sensual sensation. One that would get him in trouble if he continued, especially in front of the ranch's stables. "Call me later?"

"I will."

Garrett checked his watch. If he didn't hurry up, he'd be late for dinner. He hopped in his truck and drove across the ranch to Dylan and Emma's. Just as he took the first step up to their front porch, he heard the sound of snow crunching behind him.

Garrett spun around and lurched in its direction.

"What the hell, man?" Dylan stumbled backward, almost falling to the ground.

Garrett laughed. "Don't give me that crap, big brother.

You were going to do the exact same thing to me. I just beat you to it."

"Shut up." Dylan punched him in the arm. "I figured your head would still be in the clouds after that kiss goodbye."

Now he was the one turning red. "Didn't Mom ever tell you it's not polite to spy on people?"

"Didn't Mom ever tell you to keep the public displays of affection to a minimum?"

"Oh, you should talk. From what I heard, you practically courted Emma from the day she arrived."

"Hardly the truth. She wanted my ranch and any cordiality I had showed was because she was pregnant."

"Yeah, that the only reason?" Garrett had missed taunting his brothers while he lived in Wheatland. His life would never be the same without Rebecca, but he was realizing it was all right to enjoy what he had.

"Bet you're still slower than me." Dylan raced him up the stairs.

The front door swung wide. "Are you two going to stand out here acting like a couple of kids or are you coming in for dinner? Because if not, the four of us will eat without you."

Garrett and Dylan looked at each other and laughed. "Oh my God, I think my fiancée just channeled Mom."

"Speaking of Mom, have you heard from her lately?"

"Not since Christmas. You?" Dylan closed the door behind them as they kicked off their boots.

"It was sometime after New Year's, but not much later than that. I told her we had moved and she almost sounded disappointed that I'd come back to Saddle Ridge."

"When she left, I thought she was running from Dad's death, but it didn't take her long to sell the ranch and hook up with Artie."

"Artie is okay." Garrett shrugged off his coat. "He's not the sharpest knife in the drawer but he genuinely cares about Mom. Mom doesn't want the memories of this place and I can't blame her."

"I keep waiting for it to go back up for sale," Dylan said.

"Why? Would you really buy that place back? Ryder killed Dad there."

"Ryder accidentally ran over Dad and he died."

"They were fighting and Ryder ran him over. However you look at it, Ryder was behind the wheel and Dad died. That's a hard thing to forgive and it's even harder to forget."

"It's in the past. And it looks like the two of us have a great future ahead."

It was looking brighter every day. The pain of losing Rebecca would never fade, but he was learning how to handle it better by allowing himself to be happy again.

Maybe Cupid wasn't so bad after all.

"It's ABOUT TIME you came to see me." Liv gave Delta a hug. "And hello there, Jake." She scratched the top of his head. "I'm glad you came to see me, too."

"I'm sorry. I've just been busy between work, the convalescent home, running back and forth to see my parents and—" Delta cut herself short, not sure if she was ready to talk about Garrett to Liv, or anyone for that matter. Belle was probably the one exception to that rule, but only because Belle hadn't given her much of a choice.

"Oh, no you don't." Liv eased onto the couch. "You're leaving something or someone out, and I think I know who it is."

"Yeah, okay." Delta laughed. "How are you feeling? Because you look uncomfortable."

Liv swept her long, jet-black hair up off her shoulders and held it at the nape of her neck for a second before releasing it. Her hair coupled with her feline-like emerald-green eyes was striking. "I just went to the doctor today for a checkup. We're at just over a pound each. That's three pounds of kids sitting on my bladder, kicking my ribs and poking me in places I didn't know I could be poked. This could be you someday."

"I doubt that."

"How does Garrett feel about having more kids?" Liv asked.

"We haven't tal—" Delta's mouth slammed shut. "How did you know about him?"

"You two made quite the couple ice skating the other day." Liv pulled her phone out of her shirt pocket. "I don't go anywhere without this thing anymore. I never know when I won't be able to get up. Let's see." She began swiping at the phone. "The video of you two together is on here somewhere. And it's super sexy."

"Oh, my God. Please tell me you don't have a video of us ice skating together." Delta's heart thudded to a stop.

"Fine. I don't have a video. But your reaction tells me something sexy did happen. Dish. Now."

"I will not. But he told me to tell you hello."

"Hello back. Have his boots been under your bed yet?" Liv waggled her brows.

"You are incorrigible!"

The doorbell rang and Maddie, who lived next door, walked in. "I saw your Jeep out front. Are you two having a party without me?"

Jake nudged her with his nose. "Excuse me, fuzzy butt. My mistake. Are you *three* having a party without me?"

"Since you both are here, I have something to tell you. I just finished talking with Jade about it before you came in."

"Is your sister leaving LA and moving back to town?"

Liv scoffed. "As if. Hell would have to freeze over twice for that to happen. I know I said I was going to wait, but when I was at my appointment earlier, I asked them to tell me the sex of the babies. I just couldn't wait any longer."

"You did!" Maddie bounced up and down the same way Kacey did. Only Kacey was much cuter. "What are you having?"

"Three girls." Liv beamed. "And I've already chosen their names, because I knew in my heart of hearts that they were going to be girls. How do you like Audra, Hadley and Mackenzie?"

"I love them." Delta was over the moon thrilled for Liv. She wished they were both celebrating a baby, but she was glad for her friend.

"We need to have a toast." Liv struggled to get off the couch. "I swear I'm going to have to hire a manservant just to get me up from a seated position. It wouldn't be so bad if I hadn't chosen such comfortable furniture. Everything in this house sucks you into it."

"You can't drink."

"Relax, I'm going to have apple juice and you two are having the spiced rum. I think the bottle belonged to one of you anyway. I guess we won't be having those crazy nights anymore."

As happy as Delta was for Liv, there was a touch of sadness behind those words. She had never been pregnant, but she could see why women would wax nostalgic for their former glory days.

Liv led them to the kitchen and set three rocks glasses on the counter. She added ice, then topped two off with rum and one with juice. "Here's to girl power." She raised her glass.

"To girl power." Delta and Maddie joined her and clinked glasses before sipping their drinks. "And to Delta's new boyfriend."

"Oh, you're funny." Delta took a long swallow of rum and headed back into the living room. "Garrett and I don't know what we—ow—ouch." She dropped her glass on the coffee table.

"Delta, what's wrong?"

"It's like someone's stabbing me in the shoulder and the armpit." She exhaled sharply. "Damn."

"Sit down." Maddie ushered her to the couch. "Did you do anything extraneous today?"

"No." Delta tried rubbing her shoulder. "I had one job early this morning and that was it. The rest of the day was easy."

"Here, let me." Maddie began to rub it for her. "Does it hurt when you move?"

"I don't know. I don't remember pulling it or anything." She raised her arm in the air.

"Have you lost weight?" Maddie asked as she massaged her shoulder and under her arm. "You're always thin, but you feel thin." Her friend froze.

"What's wrong?"

Maddie's fingers dug deeper into her flesh. "Delta, I feel something under your arm."

"Oh, God." Liv covered her mouth as tears filled Maddie's eyes.

Delta shook her head. "No, no, no, no. I'm sure I just pulled something. That's all."

"Give me your hand." Maddie held out hers. "You can't ignore this. Give me your hand."

Tears filled her own eyes as Maddie guided her to the middle of her armpit and pressed her fingers into her skin. Her stomach dropped as she felt it, too. Her lymph nodes were swollen. She had lost a couple pounds but she'd figured it was from working too much. That was also why she assumed she'd been tired lately. But the alcohol intolerance pain. She'd never had the symptom originally, but she was aware it existed.

"How can this be happening? My scans were clear four months ago. I can't have Hodgkin's again. I just can't."

Chapter Eleven

Delta had left for Missoula sometime after Garrett saw her Wednesday and he still hadn't heard from her two days later. She had sent him a text message in the middle of the night stating she had a family emergency and would call when she was able to. He had been awake when the message came in, but when he immediately called her back, it went straight to voice mail.

Normally that wouldn't have concerned him. It was her outgoing message that didn't sit right. She stated she'd be out of town for a few days and she provided the name and number of another farrier. That part was straightforward. Her shakiness toward the end of the message and the hitch in her voice when she said goodbye concerned him. And when he ran into Liv Scott in the supermarket yesterday and had asked if she'd heard from Delta, the woman couldn't get away from him fast enough. Something was wrong and Garrett believed it went way beyond a family emergency.

He'd even gone as far as asking Harlan to check all the emergency rooms in Missoula County. He found nothing. Garrett stopped short of tracking down her family. She deserved to have privacy, but that didn't mean it wasn't driving him crazy.

People had family emergencies all the time. Barring a natural disaster or inclement weather, they usually got messages to people. Garrett had left several for Delta and she hadn't returned a single one. Radio silence usually meant the person didn't want to talk.

Garrett surveyed the lodge's great room. Silver Bells had officially reopened yesterday and was bustling with guests. A Montana romance writers' group, to be exact. They seemed pleasant enough. They had taken over the great room and dining areas with their laptops but had been relatively tame. So far.

"Not a bad group from the looks of it." Dylan slapped him on the back.

"Just wait until tonight," Garrett warned. "I think you'll have your hands full."

"Nah, these women will probably pack it in early. They've been working all day."

Dylan didn't give their clientele much credit. "They are definitely looking to play later. A few of them have already asked me about the nightlife here in Saddle Ridge."

"Saddle Ridge doesn't have any nightlife, unless you count the Iron Horse."

"Exactly, I told them about a few places in Kalispell, but I still think they'll end up here, asking you to entertain them."

"You mean asking us," Dylan reminded. "We're partners now. Everything is fifty-fifty, including the entertainment."

"Well my fifty percent will be home watching three

kids. I guess you forgot it's my turn to take the kids for the weekend so Belle and Harlan can have their own romantic time alone. Once the baby comes they won't have a moment's peace."

"Unless they have an angel like Holly. She hardly ever cries," Dylan mused. "I don't remember every other weekend off being a part of our partnership agreement. It's not fair to leave me to fend for myself."

"Hey, Belle and Harlan are leaving me to fend for myself."

"Yeah." Dylan scratched his chin. "You have a point there. I don't know which one of us has it worse."

"I had hoped Delta would be joining me for part of the night."

"Doesn't she usually visit her parents on the weekend?"

"Most of the time, not always." And it wasn't as if he'd even mentioned the weekend to her yet. He hadn't had the chance before she'd left with whoever she left with. He'd driven by her house. Twice. And both of her vehicles were parked around back. "Like I said, I had hoped she would join me."

"Still no word?"

Garrett shook his head.

"I won't tell you not to worry about it because we know firsthand how tragedy can strike at any minute. From the little I do know about her, she's from a very strong family and Buck Grace has always been about his kids."

"You know Delta's father?"

Dylan nodded. "It's been probably ten years, if not more. I doubt the man would recognize me. He was in town to see Henry when he shod Dad's horses. I met him on our ranch."

Garrett had no idea Delta's father had met their father, let alone on the family homestead. Not that it mattered, which just proved how small Montana really was despite its size.

According to the clock in the lobby, it was almost time to pick up Bryce and Kacey from their respective schools. Even with Emma's volunteering, he felt the inexplicable need to keep his children close.

"Good luck tonight, I need to go pick up my kids so your future wife can have a long overdue break. Watch out for some of those women. Especially the authors of some of the steamier works. I wish I could be here to watch you sing around the fire later."

"Bring the kids, that'll keep everything tame."

"Nah, man. You're on your own."

He already knew the first question out of his daughter's mouth would be about Delta. And he didn't have any answers. He had already noticed Kacey's demeanor backsliding. Delta hadn't spoken to her since Tuesday night. She never dropped off the guitar either, which Garrett was fine with, but Kacey was struggling to understand Delta's absence wasn't about her, and that they had to pray everything would be okay.

It had to be.

"OKAY, DELTA." Dr. Lassiter sat behind his desk Friday afternoon at the Montana Cancer Center in Missoula. "We have the results of all your scans and the fine needle aspiration we took this morning."

Delta's parents sat on either side of her, squeezing

her hands tightly, while her two brothers stood behind her for support. She already knew what he was going to say. She'd seen that look on Dr. Lassiter's face before.

"How bad?"

"Delta, don't assume the worst." Her mother attempted to comfort her.

"Stage Ia favorable. Meaning it's not bulky or in several different lymph node areas like it was the last time. Based on your scan and blood test results, I feel your fatigue and slight weight loss has been environmental and not medical. We caught this early. But—"

"Oh, God. It hurts me to hear this. It's never good when you say *but*." Her mother started fanning herself.

"Erma Jean, give the man a chance to speak." Her father turned to Trevor. "Keep her calm, will you."

"As I was saying." Her oncologist cleared his throat. "You have classic Hodgkin's lymphoma and it is highly curable because we caught it so early. You'll receive two cycles of ABVD chemotherapy, which is four treatments over the course of eight weeks, followed by ISRT, or involved site radiation therapy. You should experience fewer side effects with this course of treatment. But, Delta, I cannot stress enough that this is nothing like the last time. It's going to be difficult at times, but we will get you through this."

She wanted to cry foul. She wanted to scream. She wanted to punch something. It was bad enough to go through it once, but twice made her want to throw up her hands, look skyward and say, "What gives?" She'd never been the *why me* type of person. But twice?

And she knew—she knew other people battled far worse many more times than she had. They would be envious of her diagnosis. It was treatable. That alone made her feel guilty. She was entitled to the anger. If she held on to it, she wouldn't cry.

She wanted her pre-cancer life back. She wanted her home and her husband and the kids they had planned to have. Cancer had robbed her of that future and it had robbed Garrett of his. He was right. Cancer was selfish. How could she have even thought about getting involved with Garrett and his children. They all deserved better. It was hard enough battling cancer for yourself. It was harder when your loved ones watched you suffer through it, and you saw their pain every time they looked at you. She loved her mother, but it was easier when her mother wasn't by her side. Erma Jean wasn't strong enough. And Delta was tired of being strong for everybody else.

Trevor gently squeezed her shoulders from behind. She took a deep breath and exhaled slowly. The initial shock was out of her system. She wouldn't complain, no matter how much that pained her. Cancer sucked.

"When do I start chemotherapy?"

"Considering your history, tomorrow. Unlike last time, you will not have to return the following day to receive a chemo shot. We're using an on-body injector that will adhere to your skin and automatically administer the shot the following day so you can go home, go about your routine as much as you can. Your side effects may not be as great this time. They may be completely different."

"Will she lose her hair again?" her mother asked.

"It varies from person to person. This is lower-dose chemotherapy, so she may not lose all of it."

"That will be attractive." Delta attempted some levity.

This time she wouldn't allow cancer to take her hair. She would take it. This time she would wield the power. It was on her terms. She rubbed her forehead. She needed to hire help, an apprentice at least to help her on the days she couldn't do her job. She couldn't run a business throwing up every five minutes. She hoped the doctor was right and the side effects were less, but she had to prepare for the worst.

She also had to keep this to herself. She trusted Maddie and Liv, along with her family. If her customers found out she had cancer, she'd lose their business. Some of them already treated her differently because she was a woman. She couldn't afford any more losses. And she couldn't lose her biggest client. Knowing Garrett, he would coddle her and insist on hiring another farrier. No. Cancer would not take her life away again.

"Okay. So, uh, I guess I'll be here tomorrow to uh, do this one more time."

Delta rose from her chair, willing her legs to support her. She held out her hand to her doctor. "At least I have one of the best on my team. Thank you, Dr. Lassiter."

He covered her hand with both of his. "We will beat this, Delta."

She swallowed back the tears threatening to break free. She didn't want to cry in front of her mother and she couldn't cry in front of her father for fear they would start crying, too. She wanted to go home. To her dog. She just wanted to put this day behind her and start over tomorrow. And Dr. Lassiter was right, she would beat this. She would kick its ass all the way to the moon.

A FEW HOURS later, Delta lay on her old bed with Jake's head on her chest. She felt like a teenager waiting to be grounded. She didn't want to sit upstairs in the bedroom. She wanted to do something to get her mind off what was about to happen. But she was stuck. When she'd called her parents Wednesday night and told them about the pain and the lump, her brothers drove up from Missoula to get her. Her family was afraid she would be too upset to drive, and in hindsight, she had been. She wanted to at least go downstairs and watch television but she couldn't stand the way her parents looked at her. The pity, the sadness—everything she didn't need right now. She didn't want to wallow. She wanted to take control. She was thirty years old and stuck in her childhood bedroom.

She grabbed her phone from the night table and texted her brothers.

GET ME OUT OF HERE!

She knew they would come. She didn't care what they did or where they went. As long as they treated her normally. She hated winters in Montana. It was too cold to do anything. If it had at least been spring, she could've clipped a leash on Jake and gone for a walk into town or let Jake run in their horse pastures. She would have loved to take one of her own horses for a ride, but her mother would probably track her down and start following her five minutes later. Still, at least she would've gotten out of the house. She knew her parents meant well, it was just a little overwhelming at times.

Her phone rang and she answered it without even looking at the display. "Hello?"

"Delta, thank God. I've been trying to reach you for two days."

Delta buried her face in the pillow and screamed. She finally had a shot with a nice guy and she had to walk away. At least until she was cancer free.

"I didn't mean to worry you." She truly hadn't. In the back of her mind, she had hoped he would walk away from her and make things easier on them both. "I'm just dealing with some private family matters. I should be back to work on Monday, barring any further complications."

"I don't care about work." She sensed the annoyance in his voice. "What complications? Are you okay? Is your family okay?"

"Everything will be fine. I just needed to get home. Please tell Kacey I'm sorry for missing her guitar lessons. Is Lightning Bug still doing okay or have you had to call in the other farrier for anything?"

"Kacey will survive, she's asked about you. Everyone has asked about you. The horses are fine. And no, we haven't had to call anyone else. Why are both of your vehicles at your house? How did you get to Missoula?"

"You were at my house?" Delta wasn't sure how she felt about that. Part of her was mad that he had encroached on her personal space, the other part was touched at the amount of concern he had for her.

"My brothers picked me up."

"And that's it?"

"That's it, Garrett."

"Did something happen between us? I thought we

were headed in a positive direction but I'm sensing...
I don't know what I'm sensing from you but it almost
sounds like you're having second thoughts."

Delta closed her eyes. She didn't want to hurt him.
She didn't want to turn him away. Out of all the people in the world, she'd love nothing more than to curl
up with him and hear him say everything would be all
right. But she couldn't ask that of him. Not after what
he had been through. She wouldn't be that selfish.

"You told me the other day that if this didn't work
out, we could go back to just being friends." She pinched
the bridge of her nose, not wanting to say what had to
come next. "I thought about it and I'm just not comfortable with us dating. I think we're much better as
friends. I have no problem helping you with the Valentine's event and I'll continue to be there for Kacey,
but what happened the other day between us can't happen again."

"And here I had always been told absence made the
heart grow fonder."

"I'm sorry, Garrett. I know this isn't what you want
to hear. I just don't see it working out between us. We
don't really know each other anyway. Maybe down the
road things will be different."

"Did you seriously just give me the 'let's just be
friends' speech and then hint we might have a chance
later on? What am I supposed to do, wait for you?"

Yes. "I would never ask you to do that. I'm just not
ready for a relationship. I thought I was, but I'm not."

There was a soft knock at her bedroom door. "Delta,
it's Cooper."

"I'm sorry, Garrett, I have to go. My brother just arrived."

"Yeah, sure. Goodbye, Delta."

His words pierced her heart more painfully than any arrow ever could.

"The door's open."

Cooper strode in and flopped on the bed beside her just as he had when they were kids. Her brother was one year older than her and every bit as much a cowboy as he was a deputy sheriff. Harlan reminded her of him in many ways. Under different circumstances, the two of them would probably get along famously. But she didn't want anyone from Garrett's family involved with hers. She needed that separation.

"What's going on, chickadee?" He reached down and squeezed her hand. "Mom and Dad getting to you?"

"Everything's getting to me." Her brothers were the only people she could rely on to keep her sane. And she could trust them like no tomorrow. Jake may be her rock, but they were her foundation.

"Why don't you get your things and come stay with Trevor and me at the apartment tonight. I know Mom and Dad will want to take you to chemo tomorrow, but that's your decision. If it's too difficult having them there, then I'll say something so you won't have to."

"I don't know. I don't want to hurt Mom's feelings and tell her she can't go, but I don't want her stressed out for hours either. She'll look at people sicker than I am and think the worst is going to happen to me." Delta shook her head. "It was one thing when we went through this the first time. I'm not as sick, but they still have to pump poison through my body, which is the real reason why I called you over here. I need you to do me a favor. And I need it tonight."

Chapter Twelve

"Are you sure you want to do this?" Cooper stood behind her in his apartment bathroom on the other side of town from their parents' house. "The doctor said you may not lose all of it."

"What am I supposed to do? Go around looking like a patchwork quilt or buy some of that spray-on hair?" In the mirror, she saw the anguish in his eyes at what she had asked him to do. "It's okay. This isn't my first rodeo. The last time I went through chemo I bawled every time it fell out in clumps. I'm not going through that again. This is a good thing." She attempted a smile. "I still have my old wig. Shit, that thing cost almost five thousand dollars. And it's real hair. No one is going to know except our immediate family. I want to walk into that cancer center tomorrow and spit in cancer's face."

"I love you, sis."

"I love you, too."

Cooper gathered her hair in a low ponytail and tied it with an elastic band. She handed him the scissors from the bathroom vanity and nodded, reassuring him it was okay. In three swift cuts, what was left of her hair fell forward and framed her face. She continued to stare at her reflection. Part one...done. He handed her the pony-tail. She took a deep breath before wrapping her finger around what used to be her hair.

They had downloaded the form from *Locks of Love* and would send in her hair along with a donation so they could create a hairpiece for a child suffering from medical hair loss. This way she didn't lose her hair to chemo. She willingly gave it to someone in need.

Take that, cancer!

"Are you sure you don't want to leave it like this?" Cooper asked. "I can take you somewhere and you can get a pixie cut. It will look cute."

Delta lifted her chin. "Do it, Cooper."

Her brother switched on the hair clippers and wiped away a lone tear before making the first pass across her scalp. She watched as he shaved every hair from her head, leaving her completely bald. Part two...done.

Screw you, cancer!

HER MOM WEPT when Cooper and Trevor brought her home after her first three-hour chemo treatment. She probably should have warned her about the hair.

"Do you want to lay down?" her father asked.

"Not yet. The anti-nausea drugs they gave me seem to be working okay."

"Do you want something to eat?" her mother asked.

"I'm good, Mom." Now food was a trigger. She inhaled sharply. The thought alone made her feel queasy. "Let's not talk about food."

"Mom, Dad." Trevor guided her to the couch as if she had broken a leg or some other body part. "Just leave her alone and let her rest."

"Yo, bro." Delta looked up at him. "You can let go of my arm now. I'm not going to fall apart. I got this. But if you don't mind, could you grab me a bucket just in case and that bag of sour hard candies I left in the car."

ABVD chemo consisted of a noxious cocktail of four different drugs. Adriamycin, Bleomycin, Vinblastine and Dacarbazine. Adriamycin, also known as The Red Devil, attacked the cancer the hardest. It also turned urine frighteningly red and tasted like the devil's butt crack. Hard candy helped mask the taste, the stronger the better. Not much was stronger than kid's sour candy. It was vile on a good day, but a lifesaver during and after chemo.

"Are you sure you don't need anything?" Mom hovered nearby with a dish towel in one hand and a glass of water in the other.

"Mom, what are you doing?" She shook her head. "If it will make *you* feel better, give me the towel and the water."

Delta tucked the towel into the front of her sweatshirt and held the glass of water in her lap. Cooper had returned from the kitchen with chipmunk cheeks full of food. He was trying his best not to eat in front of her, but she knew he was hungry.

"Why are you wearing a towel?" he asked.

"It makes Mom feel better."

"What exactly is that doing for you?"

"Nothing, but I figured if I start drooling, I'm covered."

He sat down next to her on the couch and wrapped his arm around her shoulders as he turned on the television. "Comedy or horror?"

"Horror." She flipped up her hoodie and rested her head against him, relishing his warmth. It was one thing to be bald in the South, it was an entirely different animal being bald in northwestern Montana, in the middle of winter. "Horror means they won't try to slip a romance in there."

The last thing Delta remembered was the sound of a chain saw.

IT HAD BEEN six days since Garrett had last seen Delta. As much as he had tried to erase her from his thoughts, he couldn't. It didn't help that Kacey had continued to ask about her. Their breakup, or whatever she wanted to call it, still didn't make sense to him. Neither did her absence.

Garrett crested the hill in front of the stables on his four-wheeler on Tuesday as Delta entered Silver Bells' main gate. A part of him wanted to ride over and see how she was doing, but the other part told him to keep his distance. He could see her clearly enough from where he was. He didn't need to get any closer. Providing she had all her limbs intact, that was all that mattered. Whatever her emergency was, she didn't want to talk about it and he didn't need to know.

Another truck he hadn't seen before braked next to hers. No one parked at the stables unless they had business there and he had never seen the man who stepped out of the vehicle. But Delta had. Even from a distance, he could tell they knew each other well. Maybe a little too well. Was that why she'd ended things with him? Was it because of someone else?

He pushed the thumb throttle forward and rolled

down the hill toward them. The stables were his business and he had a right to know who was entering them. He idled to a stop in front of them and cut the engine.

"Good afternoon, Delta." He tipped his hat to her and climbed off the four-wheeler before holding his hand out to the man who appeared much younger in person than he had from a distance. He couldn't be more than twenty years old, if that. "I don't believe we've met."

"I'm Evan, Delta's apprentice."

"Apprentice?" Garrett hadn't realized Delta had become busy enough to hire someone else. He also didn't remember her looking so pale or her hair being that particular shade of brown. It was a pretty color, but Delta didn't have that much mahogany in hers. Something was off.

Delta shifted uncomfortably under his gaze, quickly averting her eyes. "It was time for me to hire someone. It's the perfect time of year to get him up to speed while we're a little bit slower. Come spring, we'll be ready to shift into high gear and take on more clients."

Now Garrett felt like a complete fool for thinking the man was anything other than a legitimate employee. Delta wouldn't bring a man she was dating on the job. And he could tell himself he was over her all he wanted. He could tell himself they'd never had anything to begin with, but that would be a lie, too. And he could tell himself he didn't care anymore when the truth was he cared enough to know something was wrong.

"I'm available to give Kacey a guitar lesson later, if it's still okay."

"She would be thrilled if you're sure it's not a problem."

"I can't guarantee a schedule, if that's what you're

getting at, but I'm pretty sure I can fit her in once, if not twice a week. I brought my travel guitar with me. I'm sorry our lesson plans got interrupted, but life happened."

"I'm leaving in a few to pick her and Bryce up. How long do you plan on sticking around?"

"I'm just showing Evan the ranch today. We're not working, so I can wait until you get home. I have nothing after this."

"Okay, I won't be long. Meet me at the house?"

Delta nodded before returning her attention to Evan.

Garrett had a sinking feeling when he walked away from her. It wasn't just the hair and her complexion. That special spark she'd always had in her eyes was missing. And maybe it was because of what happened between them, but instinct and experience told him it was much more.

Less than a half hour later, his SUV had barely stopped in front of the house before Kacey was yanking off her seat belt and attempting to open the door to jump out.

"Delta!" She dropped her backpack in the snow and ran into her open arms. "I missed you."

"I missed you, too. I'm sorry I wasn't around, I had to take care of something back home."

"I thought this was home."

"I have two homes, sweetheart. One here and one with my parents. I go back and forth between the two."

"Your hair looks pretty," Kacey said. His daughter had just confirmed his suspicions.

"Thank you." Delta ran her hand over the back of it. "I had it done when I was visiting my family."

Garrett furrowed his brow. Could he possibly be reading too much into her absence? It wasn't unusual for a woman to get a cut and color. And he hadn't been around her long enough to know what her usual style was.

"Did you bring the guitar?" Kacey attempted to look behind Delta.

"Yes I did. I know you were expecting it last week, but I had to leave for a few days."

"Can I see it?"

"Why don't we all go inside first?" Garrett held Bryce's hand as his son climbed the stairs.

He unlocked the door so the kids could go in ahead of them. "Delta." He reached for her arm before she entered the house. "I know it's none of my business, but are you okay?"

"Everything is fine, Garrett."

"I'm not asking you about everything. I'm asking about you." The closer he got to her, the more he was almost positive she was wearing a wig. The average person wouldn't have noticed it. But he'd had his hands in her hair before. He knew what it looked like. He knew what it smelled like. He knew how it fell across her shoulders. He knew the way she wore it parted. Everything he knew wasn't what he was seeing. "Despite what did or didn't happen between us, I'm still your friend. I made you that promise and I won't break it. If you want to talk, I'm here."

"I appreciate it, but it's not necessary. Thank you anyway."

"Delta! Are you coming?"

She looked to him for permission. "The question

is, are you still okay with me spending time with your kids?"

"As long as you don't break their hearts."

"I wouldn't think of it."

"Just so you know, Dylan had tried teaching her to play and it didn't go so well."

"Why not?"

"He wasn't you."

"KACEY, WHAT DO YOU say to Delta?" Garrett asked after her lesson.

"Thank you. I will take very good care of it until I get my own guitar." Kacey looked up at him with her big doe eyes. "I will get one, won't I?"

"Maybe Santa Claus will bring you one."

"Santa? Christmas is a long way away."

"You don't want to wait that long? Hmm." Garrett tapped his temple. "I wonder what kind of occasion would call for a gift like a guitar."

"Kacey's birff-day!" Bryce shouted from the kitchen table. "Right, Kacey?"

"I don't know what he's talking about." Kacey feigned innocence. "But maybe that's a good idea."

"We'll see. You have to be a good girl in the meantime."

Delta closed the guitar case and stood it against the fireplace before grabbing her tote bag. "I hate to cut out on you already, but Jake and I have to get to a birthday party at the convalescent home."

"Can I go with you?" Kacey asked.

"If it's okay with your father." Delta looked over his daughter's head at him.

"Thanks for putting me on the spot." He narrowed his eyes. "I think there's too much sadness there."

"Daddy, have you been there before?" Kacey asked. "How is a birthday party sad?"

Delta crossed the room to him. "It might be good for her to see that not all sick people die," she whispered.

"Yeah, sometimes they just struggle silently without realizing there are people around them who truly care," he bit out in return.

Delta's body physically stiffened at his remark.

"Kacey, honey." Garrett refused to break eye contact with Delta. "Go clean up if you're going to a party."

"Yay, I'm going to a party! I'm going to a party!" Kacey sang as she ran out of the room. "I'm going with you, Jake."

"You can take her with you." Garrett leaned closer to her. "But if I lower my guard for you, then I expect you to do the same. You can hide your secret from everyone else...not me. I know. And I'll wait patiently for you to tell me the entire story. I'll wait."

"You don't know a thing about it."

"I know everything about it. I know the devastation. I know the pain. I know the sickness. And I know you need support now more than ever."

"I washed my hands and face, Daddy."

"Did you brush your teeth?" he asked. Bryce climbed off his chair and ran into the bathroom.

"I'm going to the potty," he mimicked his sister and slammed the door.

"Bryce, let your sister in there. She needs to go." Garrett chased after him and jiggled the doorknob. It was locked.

"I'm going to the potty," Bryce continued to sing from the other side of the door, followed by the sound of trickling water and a flush. He heard the wooden step in front of the toilet scrape across the floor, and then the basin faucet turn on.

"Apparently I have one going to a party and the other going to the potty." Garrett leaned against the doorjamb waiting for his son to emerge.

The knob jiggled and then the door opened. "I went to the potty." Bryce shuffled past the three of them in stocking feet and climbed back into the chair.

Garrett clapped his hands loudly. "Good job, buddy, but stop locking the door. Kacey, teeth, now. Delta, we're talking later when you return."

"Fine."

"Fine."

DELTA FELT PHYSICALLY sick during their drive into town, but it wasn't from the chemo. Cooper had driven her home Sunday morning and had stayed until early Monday before heading straight to work. Out of the three of them, her older brother was the most even-keeled and self-disciplined. As a former marine, he didn't back down from a fight. His *oorah* battle cry had carried her through her last trip to hell and back and she welcomed it again this time. She needed to call on that battle cry tonight to get through her talk with Garrett later. She was a fool to think she could hide her diagnosis from someone who had lived with the scars it left behind.

Sensing her anxiety, Jake rested his head in her lap the entire way there. They pulled into a full parking lot and circled twice before finding a spot large enough for her work truck. She wished she'd had a chance to go home and change first, but she'd only worked on one horse earlier. Evan had done the rest under her supervision.

The bone pain that accompanied the after-chemo injection made working almost unbearable. When her father's connections had led Evan to her door Monday morning, she welcomed his assistance. He was just what the doctor ordered. Literally.

Delta clipped a leash on Jake and held the hand loop open for Kacey. "Slip this over your wrist and hold on to him tight. You wait for me while I get my stuff."

Guitar in one hand, bag over her shoulder, kid with dog in the other hand. How did parents do it when there were other children added to the mix? She was out of arms and so was her assistant kid. She couldn't even fathom how Liv would manage three infants at the same time. But her friend was making sure she was prepared for every possible scenario. If there was a class, video or book about multiples, she had it.

The party was in full swing when they entered the home's dining area. Parties usually occurred on the weekend, but today was Ralph's hundred-and-second birthday. He refused to have it on the weekend for fear he wouldn't live long enough to make the celebration. Every year, he threw himself a party, invited all the residents and staff, and footed the catering bill.

"Happy birthday, Ralph." She gave the man a hug as she walked in the room.

"My precious Delta." He held her face in his hands. "I'm so happy you joined us tonight." He bent forward and petted Jake before smiling at Kacey. "Who is this beautiful princess?"

"I'm Kacey." She hugged the man. "Happy birthday."

"Thank you." Ralph hugged her in return. "Oh, to be young again."

Kacey talked to everyone. It didn't matter if they acknowledged her or not. She smiled and introduced herself around the room with Jake close by her side. Delta wanted to believe Kacey was babysitting her dog, but the way Jake constantly kept her eyes in his line of vision told her he was the primary caretaker.

Delta had her guitar out when Kacey rejoined them carrying two paper plates full of food. "Mr. Ralph gave these to me. He's a hundred and two. How many times older is he than me?"

"Almost thirteen, I think." Delta helped her set both plates on the table.

"Wow."

Wow was right. Hopefully they'd all live to be that age and still be happy. "Thank you for bringing me dinner, sweetheart. You're a terrific little helper."

"I thought Jake was gonna eat it before I got to the table. Who is that man?" Kacey looked toward the sunroom entrance. "He keeps looking at you and smiling."

"That's Joe. He's one of the permanent residents here. Funny as the day is long. He'll have you rolling on the floor laughing at his stories." Delta lowered her voice and leaned closer to Kacey. "He thinks he's God's gift to women, though."

"Isn't he a little old for you?" Kacey wrinkled her nose.

"In his mind, he'll always be in his twenties. He's

harmless." Delta took a bite of her chicken-and-grape-salad croissant. Her appetite had returned yesterday, but her taste buds were still a little off.

"He walks like Aunt Belle's rooster."

Delta almost choked on a grape. "That he does."

"Daddy's been really sad without you around. He misses you."

"I was only gone for a little while."

"Almost a whole week." She pouted. "He had to work on that Valentine's Day thingy by himself."

With all the cancer crap going on, she had completely forgotten about the couples-only retreat. She'd given him all the information she'd had, but it was a huge undertaking for one person. The event started in four days and she hoped he'd used all her contacts.

"I'll see if I can help him when we get to the house." If he still wanted her help after the way she'd treated him.

"I'll help, too." Kacey nodded her head matter-of-factly. "You and Daddy need all the help you can get."

If that wasn't the truth, Delta didn't know what was.

"THANK YOU FOR coming over." Garrett greeted Dylan on the front porch two hours after Delta had dropped off Kacey. "They are already in bed. I'll be back before they ever realize I'm gone."

"Take your time and don't race over there and get yourself killed along the way." Dylan didn't ask why he needed a sudden babysitter, but he had rightfully assumed it was because of Delta. "Emma and Holly are already asleep, too, so it's not like anyone's missing me.

And if you don't come back tonight, I'll just tell the kids you had an early errand and I'll drive them to school."

"That's not going to happen." Garrett clapped his brother on the back. "But thanks for the offer."

He descended the porch steps two at a time, almost slipping on the last one.

"I hope you're planning on driving better than you walk," Dylan called after him. "You have two kids counting on you to return in one piece."

Garrett hesitated before getting in his SUV. Was going over to see Delta the right thing to do? She had refused to talk to him with the kids in earshot and had promised to discuss it later. He couldn't wait for later. He needed to know what she was hiding, although in his heart he already knew her cancer had returned.

Fifteen minutes later he idled to a stop alongside her Jeep in front of her house. The dashboard clock glowed quarter after ten. Okay, so it was late, but not exactly super late. The lights were on inside her house, and if he saw movement, then he'd knock on the door. If he didn't, then he would head home.

His phone rang loudly in the darkness of the truck, almost causing him to jump out of his seat. It was Delta's number.

"Hello."

"Are you just going to sit out there all night, or are you going to come in?"

"I guess you heard me pull up." Garrett's gaze moved from one window to the next, expecting to see her watching him.

"It's a quiet ranch in the middle of the night and your

truck has an exhaust leak," she ground out through what sounded like clenched teeth.

"It does not."

Delta sighed. "Are you going to argue with me or are you going to come in?"

"I'll be right there."

Garrett's hand rested on the door handle as he braced himself for whatever she had to tell him. No matter how bad it was, he could handle it.

Delta wordlessly opened the door as he reached the top step and Jake ran out to happily greet him.

"I'm sorry for coming over here so late."

She patted her thigh and Jake immediately returned to her side. "No you're not, but if it makes you feel better to say that, then so be it."

"Wow, okay. You don't mince words, do you?" Why was he the one getting attitude? She was the one who'd disappeared and then ended things abruptly. Not him.

"No, I don't. I have cancer again."

Garrett grabbed the door frame to steady himself from the onslaught of her words. He hadn't even made it all the way into the house. "I thought so." His legs felt like they were weighted down with cement as he finished stepping over the threshold and closed the door behind him. "How bad?" His heart thumped so loud in his ears he doubted he'd hear her response.

"Nowhere near last time." She turned and trudged into the living room, motioning for him to follow her.

For the next hour, Delta painstakingly described the events of the previous week. When she finished she waited in silence while he processed the information.

Hearing the words come out of her mouth made it

all that much more real. It bothered him that she had thought he was so damaged from Rebecca's death that she had to hide the truth from him. He respected her reasons for not wanting to tell anybody else. While he would never deem her less capable of doing her job, he could see where others might.

He wanted to ask how this could happen again, but he already knew the answer. He wanted to ask how she was feeling, but he already knew that answer, too. Despite the defiant tilt of her chin, her delicate features screamed loneliness and fear.

"I wish you had trusted me enough to tell me sooner instead of trying to hide it from me."

"I didn't want you to go through this again."

"Sweetheart, it's not the same thing. You don't have pancreatic cancer. You have a ninety-five percent survival rate. It's going to be okay." He drew her into his arms and held her close. "Everything's going to be okay."

INSTEAD OF LEAVING like she had expected him to, Garrett had lit a fire and they watched the flames dance in the darkness while they snuggled together beneath a tangled mass of blankets from the couch. Jake stretched out on the floor beside them, lifting his head only when he heard the rustle of the snack-chip bags they had dug out of the kitchen pantry an hour ago.

Somewhere between channel surfing and mischievous childhood stories, they had settled into the most passionate make-out session of her life. Which Garrett had abruptly ended fifteen minutes ago. He had checked the time on his phone no less than ten times since then.

His body became more rigid with each passing second, making her more nervous. "Okay, cowboy." She flipped the blankets off them and stood in front of him. "It's time to call it a night. And don't argue with me. I know you need to get home to relieve Dylan."

"I don't want to go." He tugged at the hem of her flannel shirt. "My brother's okay with watching the kids all night. He said so before I left. But I should at least text him and let him know I'm staying. Unless you want me to go."

"You're sure he doesn't mind?" Delta couldn't deny wanting him to stay. Now that she had told him the truth, she felt a thousand times freer. She had suspected Garrett would be understanding, she just hadn't wanted to put him through the agony of watching another woman fight for her life.

"Absolutely."

"So why don't you send him that text, then."

Delta began slowly unbuttoning her shirt as he typed out his message.

"What are you doing?" His eyes grew wide in the firelight as he watched her.

"I'm waiting for you to hit Send and put your phone away." She slid the shirt from her shoulders, leaving her wearing only a pink satin bra and black thermal leggings. "Do you want me with or without?"

"With or without what?" He perched on the edge of the couch.

"Choose one and you'll find out."

"Without."

Delta reached behind her and unfastened her bra, allowing it to fall to the floor. His gaze upon her bare breasts empowered her to continue her seduction. He reached for her hand, but she took a step backward.

"Now, now." She waggled a finger at him. "Patience is a virtue. With or without."

"Please, without." He groaned, reclining against the back of the couch once again.

She hooked her thumbs in the waistband of her leggings and eased them past her hips. Reveling in the warmth of the fire against her bare skin. She stepped out of her pants and stood before him, with only a slip of lace shielding his view from the rest of her.

"With or without?"

"Without." His voice was barely a whisper.

She swung her hips as the lace slid down her hips and onto her thighs, before releasing and allowing it to fall the rest of the way. She stood naked in front of him, allowing him to see every inch, every scar, every imperfection.

His piercing gaze met hers. "You still have one more to go."

Delta laughed. "I can't get more naked than this." She knelt in front of him. "Unless you mean this." She reached for his belt and began to unfasten it. His hand covered hers, stilling it.

"Ask me again."

She could play this game all night. "With or without?"

Garrett rose before her, guiding her to her feet as his eyes roamed the entire length of her body once again. He held her face in his hands and kissed her mouth lightly before whispering, "I want you without." His fingers slid toward her scalp and under the edge of her wig, releasing the band.

"Garrett!" She tried to pull away from him but his arm wound around her waist and tugged her to him. "Don't do this."

"Without." His voice was as firm as his body against hers. She stilled in his arms. "I want you, every inch of you, naked, raw, bare. I want to see you. Not the pretense of you. It's just hair, Delta. It offers no protection, at least not from me. I want you without."

Delta sucked in a breath and closed her eyes as he continued to remove her final covering.

"You're so beautiful, Delta Grace. Embrace that beauty when you're around me."

Delta ran a hand over what used to be her hair. "I asked Cooper to do it. And I'll ask him again this weekend since it's starting to grow back. It's going to fall out and I refuse to let that happen. I took control." Once she'd arrived home last week, she'd shaved the rest of her body, with the exception of her eyebrows. She hadn't lost them completely the last time and she hoped she could fill them in with pencil again if need be.

"I love you bare." Garrett cupped the back of her head and claimed her mouth as his tongue sought hers.

"Garrett." He tilted her head back, exposing her throat. He trailed kisses down the hollow of her neck until he reached her breasts. He ran his tongue over one nipple, then blew across, causing them to harden further. "Garrett, please."

"By the time I'm finished, you'll be saying those words over and over again."

Chapter Thirteen

Garrett listened to Delta's soft breaths in the darkness of her bedroom. And he hated it. He found himself counting the seconds after each exhale and then tensing when her next inhale didn't come as quickly as the last few. He'd done the same thing when Rebecca had slept next to him.

He lifted a sweaty hand to the side of his neck and checked his heart rate with two fingers against his watch. It was a steady hundred beats a minute and that was when he knew he'd made the mistake of staying.

He didn't know how to support Delta and keep her diagnosis a secret from Bryce and Kacey. They would know. They would pick up on the signs. They would ask questions and they would be afraid of losing someone else they loved. He couldn't put them through that again. He wouldn't.

Garrett bolted upright. He had to get out of there. The walls felt as if they were closing in on him. He glanced down at Delta and saw Rebecca instead.

"No, this can't be happening." He forced himself to stand.

"Garrett?" Delta rolled over and clicked on the light.

"Oh, God." It was Rebecca. She pushed aside the covers and stood. "It can't be."

"Garrett, what's wrong?" She turned to face him. "You're drenched!"

"Delta." He sighed in relief and dropped to his knees when he realized he was having a flashback. It had to be the hair, or the lack thereof. Rebecca had been as platinum as they came. There would have been no mistaking the two, even in the dark, if they had hair. "Delta... we shouldn't have done this..."

"Excuse me?" Delta grabbed a robe from the back of a chair and tied it tightly around her. "Please tell me you did not just say that."

"Delta, I'm sorry. I can't do this. I didn't realize—"

"Get the hell out of my house!" she shouted. Jake jumped on the bed and began barking wildly at him.

"Delta, please let me explain."

"Why did you even come here?" Delta stormed out of the room only to return less than a minute later with his clothes. She threw them at him, nearly taking his eye out with his belt buckle. "Get dressed," she ordered. "I gave you an out. This was exactly why I had pushed you away. But no, you had to come over here. You had to force the issue. I didn't want you around to see this. I was doing just fine on my own. You had me snowed."

Garrett tugged on his boxer briefs and jeans as Jake continued to bark. "I can't do this to my kids."

"Don't you dare use them as an excuse." She reached across the bed for Jake's collar to quiet him before continuing. "You told me they didn't have to know. We agreed that I would keep my distance on the bad days.

You can't even admit that this is about you. You're the one who can't do this. You're a coward. Now leave and don't ever come back."

DELTA SLAMMED THE front door so hard it cracked a pane of glass.

Shit!

She plastered her back against the wall and held her breath as she listened for the sound of his SUV. Why hadn't he driven away? She refused to look. She refused to give him the satisfaction because Lord knew he had his fill of satisfaction tonight. At her expense.

Jake jumped on the back of the couch and pushed his face through the curtains. His tail stood straight out and vibrated with tension. Garrett still had to be on the porch if Jake was able to see him. The cars were parked off to the side and the front door light didn't shine that far.

She heard what sounded like a door close and then the start of his engine. Within seconds, it had faded in the distance. Her body went limp as she slid down the wall to the floor...and cried. Another man had walked away from her because she had cancer. At least she had a perfect record.

Jake jumped off the couch and ran to her side. He nudged her face repeatedly with his until she met his gaze. "I'm okay, boy." She dug her fingers into his thick coat and hugged him to her. "At least I will be." Jake rested his head on her shoulders, content to remain in that one position.

She wanted to go for a run but knew her body didn't have the stamina. She wanted to hit something but didn't want to scare Jake. She wanted to scream but didn't want to frighten her landlords across the way. She wanted to throw something, but that would only make her angrier when she had to clean it up. She wanted to not have to hold it together for once. She needed a release.

Jake pressed his body closer to hers. His nose was inches from her ear allowing her to match his breathing pattern until she calmed down. It amazed her that an animal knew what she needed when the man who'd just made love to her didn't have a clue.

Even Eddie at his worst had never left her feeling used. Just unwanted. Now she had the unfortunate knowledge of both. She released Jake and pulled herself up. She needed to strip the bed and scrub any traces of him from her body. He was the one man outside of her family she thought had understood her. The one man she thought she had a future with. The man she thought she loved. If she ever saw him again it would be too soon.

An hour had passed since Delta had thrown him out and he'd returned home. Dylan had been concerned when Garrett walked in but didn't ask questions. Which was good because he didn't have any answers. He also wasn't willing to betray Delta's trust by broadcasting her illness around either. Although, he didn't think he could betray her trust any more than he had tonight. He had never meant to hurt her, especially not that way. And he was still trying to rationalize the situation.

He stood at the kitchen window and looked into the darkness. The sun would rise in less than an hour and there was no way he'd get any sleep now. Even if he wanted to, his guilt wouldn't let him.

He knew the facts. Delta's cancer was ninety-five-percent curable. Hodgkin's lymphoma was nothing like pancreatic cancer. Delta had started treatment immediately. Rebecca's cancer had already advanced before it had been detected. And it had spread by the time she began chemotherapy. The two situations were entirely different. Then why did it feel like his heart was being torn out of his chest once again?

Garrett tugged on his boots and stepped into the frigid early-morning air. Not bothering to put on a coat or gloves he made his way to the shed attached to the back of the house and unlocked it. With a flick of the switch, he flooded the backyard with light. The yard was a mess and he was low on firewood. He gathered the branches that had fallen during the last snowfall, snapped them into smaller pieces and tossed them in the kindling box on the porch. He grabbed the ax from the shed wall, stood a slab of wood on the tree stump and started swinging.

The steel head split the wood with a resounding crack. He stood another piece upright and swung again and again until his back and shoulders couldn't take it anymore. Then he gathered the wood in his arms and stacked it alongside the house.

His body ached, his hands were cold and his ears stung, but it wasn't enough to drive the anger out of his head. He was mad at Rebecca for dying. He was mad that pancreatic cancer was linked to a hereditary gene and his children had an increased chance of getting it. He was mad Delta had cancer again and he was mad for not being strong enough to support the woman he loved. The realization hit him like a Mack truck. He was in love with Delta and he had just destroyed any chance he'd ever had with her.

"Daddy?" Kacey called to him. "What are you doing out here?"

He spun around to see her silhouetted in the back-porch doorway. "Go back inside, honey. It's too cold out here. I'm just chopping some firewood before the sun comes up. I'll be in shortly."

"The sun's up and so is Bryce," she said. "I'll feed him and get him ready for school."

Garrett looked skyward. The sun hadn't quite risen above the horizon, but it was close enough. "No, baby. You will not get Bryce dressed and ready for school. That's my job." He crossed the yard and locked the ax in the shed before joining her in the doorway. "Didn't I tell you to get inside? You're letting all the heat out of the house."

After the way he'd treated her, he doubted Delta would keep Silver Bells as a customer. How could he tell his kids they would never see Delta again? Kacey had already grown attached to her and that was his fault. He should have limited contact between them, yet she'd been good for his daughter. Bryce would miss her, but he would roll with it like he rolled with everything else. Garrett didn't think he'd survive another round of Kacey retreating into her shell. She'd just begun to come into her own and be a child, and he was going to throw another wrench in her little life.

"Why aren't you wearing a coat?"

"Because Daddy's an idiot." He pulled out a kitchen chair and patted it for her to sit on. "I want to talk to you."

He sat in the chair across from her and reached for her hands. "Daddy, don't." She backed away from him. "Your hands are cold."

"I'm sorry, baby." He rubbed them against his jeans. "I need you to let me take care of your baby brother from now on. I know you're good at it, but I want to be good at it, too, and the only way I can learn is if you let me do things for him. But you may have to show me how sometimes."

"I'd be your teacher?" Her face lit up at the idea.

"Exactly." He wanted to hug her but he knew he wasn't warm enough yet. "And since I'll be learning your job, you'll have more time to play with your friends."

"And learn guitar." She slid from the chair and ran into the living room to open her guitar case. "I can't wait until my next lesson."

"About that." Garrett followed and perched on the edge of the coffee table. "I think it's best if Dylan teaches you instead of Delta."

"But I want Delta." She deadpanned him.

"Well, honey." He had planned to have this conversation later, not before school. "That's not going to be possible."

"What did you do?"

"Me?" The accusation surprised him, although it wasn't off base. "Delta has to go back and forth to visit her family more often and she won't be able to teach you anymore."

"Doesn't she want to see me?"

"Of course she does." The last thing he wanted was for his daughter to feel unwanted and unloved. "This has absolutely nothing to do with you."

He hated lying to his kid, but he refused to allow one more person to hurt her. And while he was confident Delta would never purposely hurt Kacey, the truth would devastate her.

Kacey relatched the case and pushed it away. "It's okay. I don't want to play anymore. I'm going to get dressed for school. You need to get Bryce ready."

And her walls were up once again. An eight-year-old shouldn't even know how to turn their emotions off like that. Nor should she have to tell him how to care for his son, even though she was right. The time had slipped away from him this morning and he didn't want them to be late.

Kacey disappeared down the hall to her bedroom. Today would pass and they'd get through it together. He reminded himself that he didn't need anything more than to see his kids healthy and happy. Despite the heartache of this morning, he had done the right thing by protecting them from Delta's cancer. Then why did the right thing leave him so cold and empty?

DELTA BARELY HAD the strength to drag her body out of bed Saturday morning. If she'd had her way, she would have slept until noon. But Jake's bladder and empty belly would have none of that. It had been four days since she'd kicked Garrett out of her life and she was still waiting for him to stop invading her every waking thought.

She checked her text messages and voice mail, relieved when there weren't any. Hiring an apprentice had worked out better than she had thought it would. He'd been able to handle half of her jobs and was available in case Silver Bells had a call. They hadn't and a part of her wondered if she even had them as a customer anymore. She'd like to say she didn't care, but she did. After all, they were her largest account.

She fixed a bowl of food for Jake and sat it on the floor. "Here you go, boy."

Her back ached as she stood, along with every muscle in her body. She didn't have a temperature and was chalking the pain up to chemo side effects. So much for this time being easier than the last.

She fixed a cup of coffee and had just gotten comfortable on the couch when Jake began to circle by the back door. "Are you kidding me?" she asked him. He barked a response forcing her to get back up and let him out again. "I really wish you could do all your business at the same time."

She barely had the door open before he took off down the stairs and ran across the pastures toward her landlords' house, where he'd most likely beg for his second breakfast of the day. Typical male...never satisfied.

Delta made her way back to the couch and clicked on the TV. Every channel was engrossed in one Valentine's Day activity or another. She'd always hated cupid, but now she despised the little bugger.

Today was the tenth, the first day of the Silver Bells couples-only Valentine's Day retreat and she couldn't help but wonder how her ideas had worked out. She'd put much more of her time and heart into the project than she had intended to, but she'd secretly enjoyed it.

Too bad she couldn't see the final result. As curious as she was, she wasn't curious enough to risk running into Garrett.

Jake's distant barking followed by a child's laughter drew her to the window. She peered through the curtains to see Kacey and her dog running and jumping in the pasture next to the house. She reached for the doorknob and then realized she wasn't wearing her wig. That was the last thing Kacey needed to see.

She ran to her bedroom and lifted the wig from the stand. If Kacey was out there, Garrett had to be close by. But she hadn't heard his truck. That was odd. She looked in the mirror and adjusted her hair quickly before running back through the house. The action left her breathless by the time she reached the door. She swung it wide and stepped into the cold.

Jake had a ball in his mouth and offered it to Kacey, who happily threw it for him. Delta glanced around the property, but there was no sign of Garrett.

"Kacey!" Delta called to her, causing both her and Jake to turn in her direction. "Come on inside where it's warm."

Delta's teeth chattered as she waited for them. Jake could outrun anyone, but kept pace beside Kacey. They both reached the porch panting and sweaty.

"Delta!" Kacey scampered up the steps, threw her body against Delta and hugged her. The force almost knocked her back through the door. "I've missed you so much."

"I've missed you, too." More than she had ever imagined. "Let's get inside." She broke the embrace and ushered them both into the warmth. "Where's your father?"

Kacey shrugged. "I saw Jake running from the window of my friend's house so I came out to play with him."

"Where does your friend live?"

"Over there." Kacey pointed out the window to the new housing development on the other side of the ranch.

"Does anyone know you're here?"

She shrugged again and knelt on the floor beside Jake. "I've missed you, too."

"We need to call your father and tell him where you are." Delta grabbed her phone from the living room and pulled up Garrett's contact. Her finger hesitated over the call button while she gathered her thoughts. She wanted their conversation to be as concise as possible. The less time they spoke, the better.

He answered on the first ring. "Delta, I'm so glad you called."

"Kacey is at my house."

"What? She's supposed to be at Darlene's house with Ivy. They had a sleepover party last night."

"Does Darlene live in the housing development behind mine?"

Garrett sighed into the phone. "Yes, she does."

"She said she saw Jake playing in the pastures and she decided to join him. I don't even know if anyone realizes she's missing."

Garrett swore under his breath. "Is it okay if she stays there until I get there? I can leave now."

"That's fine." Delta hit the end button before Garrett could say another word. She'd heard enough from the man to last a lifetime. Although there was a teeny tiny part of her brain that understood and might even be able to sympathize with his reaction. She'd seen enough PTSD while working with Jake to recognize he'd had a panic attack, probably stemming from the trauma of losing Rebecca and the guilt he felt for sleeping with her. And maybe if he had called her the next day to discuss it, she would have been able to forgive him. But to not own up to it…no, she couldn't accept that.

"Your daddy is on the way over to get you." Delta handed her the phone. "Why don't you call your friend and let her parents know where you are."

"I don't know the number."

"Okay." Delta tucked the phone into the pocket of her robe, which had become increasingly suffocating over the last few minutes. "Then come in the living room and watch some TV with me while we wait."

"Are you okay?" Kacey followed her to the couch and climbed on it beside her.

"I'm overly tired today. I didn't get much sleep last night."

"You look white like Mommy."

She turned to see Kacey studying her intently. Delta grabbed the remote off the table and handed it to Kacey. "I'm fine, honey, really."

Delta glanced at the clock on the DVR. It had only been five minutes since she'd called Garrett. She picked up her phone and fired off a text to Maddie: Need your help. Can you stop over? She received a reply almost instantly: On the way.

Whoever arrived first would have to take Kacey because now she was beginning to feel like she had a fever. And the damn wig…it was so much hotter than actual hair, even during a Montana winter.

"You stay here with Jake. I'll be right back."

"Okay." Kacey changed the channel to cartoons.

Delta grabbed a cold bottle of water from the fridge before heading into the bedroom. She just needed to cool off for a minute. She twisted the cap off the bottle and took a long swig of water. She set it on the dresser, then she pulled the blinds up and lifted the window sash. The cool air felt good, but not good enough. Making sure she had closed the door behind her, Delta removed her wig and laid it on the bed. "Oh, that's so much better."

Kacey's scream from the bedroom doorway nearly shattered her eardrums. Jake began barking and circling her protectively as Delta grabbed for her wig.

"You're sick," Kacey cried. "I knew it. I knew it. Just like Mommy, you're just like Mommy and you'll leave and never come back."

Delta reached for the little girl as Kacey pulled away from her. "No!"

Garrett bounded into the room. "What is going on?" He looked from Delta to Kacey and the wig. "Oh, baby. It's not like that. It's not like Mommy. Delta's not dying, I promise."

"You knew?" Tears streamed down her cheeks as she stared up at him. "You knew she was sick. How could you give her to us when she's going away."

Garrett knelt on the floor. "She's not going away."

Delta held tight to Jake's collar. This couldn't be happening. This was exactly what she had wanted to avoid. She didn't want to scare his kids. She didn't want this to affect them.

"Delta's going to die."

"No, honey." Delta released the dog, ran across the room. "I am not dying. What I have is very curable. It's called Hodgkin's lymphoma. See, it doesn't even have cancer in the name."

"You don't have cancer?" Kacey's sobs quieted.

"I—I do, but not that kind of cancer." Delta reached out for the bed. Jake ran to her side and began barking again. When did the room begin to spin? She bent forward and almost fell to the floor. "Garrett."

"Daddy, what's happening?"

DELTA STRUGGLED TO open her eyes. There was something in her nose and around her ears. *Open your eyes!* She silently screamed. *Blink.* White. *Blink.* Bright. Ceiling. She needed to turn her head. Her brain wasn't cooperating with her body. *Come on! Fight harder!* She felt her head move slightly. *Blink.* Machines. *Shit!* She was in the hospital.

"Delta?" Maddie's voice pierced the darkness. "Delta, can you hear me?"

Delta nodded, at least she thought she did.

"Garrett?"

"I'm sorry, sweetie. He's not here."

"How?"

"You're running a fever, you have an infection and you passed out at home. He called an ambulance. There's no easy way to tell you this, but I think your secret is out."

"Where's Jake and Kacey?"

"Jake's still at your house. I'm going back there after I leave to get his food and treats. I'll take him home with me and watch him until you're released. And Kacey is with Garrett."

Maddie sighed. "I don't know how much you remember, but she saw you pass out."

Delta wanted to cry, but once again her body betrayed her and wouldn't listen.

Maddie pulled an envelope out of her bag. "Garrett asked me to give this to you. You can read it later or I can read it to you now."

"No." It didn't matter what it said. The result was the same. They were over. "Destroy it."

"You don't want me to do that."

"Destroy. Now." Delta reached for the bedrails and pressed the button.

"What are you trying to do? Sit up?" Maddie pressed the button embedded on the rail and the head of the bed began to rise.

"Stop," Delta ordered.

"How are we doing?" A nurse entered the room. "You buzzed for me."

"Please leave." Delta looked at Maddie. "Give her the letter."

"Delta, are you throwing me out?"

Delta nodded. "Please."

"Yeah, sure." She handed the letter to the nurse and slung her bag over her shoulder. "Oh, and I called your parents. They're on the way. I'll check in on you tomorrow."

"Do you want me to read this to you?" the nurse asked.

"Burn it," Delta said.

"I can't do that, but I can run it through the paper shredder if that's what you want."

"Please destroy it."

"Okay. Here, let me lower this for you so you can sleep." The bed reclined once again and Delta managed to roll over and face the wall.

She'd rather be alone than go through the pain of the last twenty-four hours. If only chemo could mend a broken heart.

Chapter Fourteen

Two days had passed since the day Delta collapsed in front of Kacey. Leaving her had been the second hardest thing of his life. The first had been burying his wife. Delta's body had taken quite a beating from the infection she'd picked up after her first round of chemo. They had released her from the hospital the following day but he didn't know any further details. After her friends and family had realized why he had ended their relationship, they refused to talk to him. And he couldn't blame them. He'd wronged her in the worst possible way. He just hoped she'd read the letter he'd written explaining why he'd done what he did and how it had been the biggest mistake of his life. He had wanted to tell her in person, but the hospital had strict orders to keep him out of her room.

Once Kacey had gotten over her initial shock at Delta's diagnosis, she began asking about her again. So had Bryce, although he was still too young to fully understand. They wanted him to call her, but he didn't want to push her further away. If she had read his letter and didn't call, he had his answer. If she hadn't read it, that was still a clear answer.

Garrett led one of the horses out of the main stables and into the middle one. They had a roof leak and needed to get in that stall. He was surprised to see Delta's truck parked in front of the building with the back open and the forge blazing. At least that was a good sign she was feeling better and they might be able to salvage some part of their relationship. He turned the corner and almost smacked into Buck Grace's chest. He was much more imposing in person than he was in his online seminars.

He grunted a greeting. An actual grunt. That wasn't a good sign.

"Mr. Grace."

"Weasel."

"Excuse me?"

"You heard me." Buck strode past him and fired a shoe. Blazing red-hot, he held it up in front of him—or maybe he was holding it up in front of Garrett as a warning—he then examined it before lowering it to the anvil and striking it with a rounding hammer. He checked it again before thrusting it back into the forge. "I'm only here because Delta has a business reputation to protect. And since you went around telling the whole damn county she has cancer, she started losing customers."

"But I didn't tell—"

"It's not your turn to talk," Buck warned. He removed the shoe from the forge with large tongs, strode to the horse, lifted the foot and set the shoe. Steam rose off the hoof, creating a smooth surface between the two. Buck finished nailing the shoe before returning his attention to Garrett. "It takes a little man to do what you've done."

"I explained everything in my letter in hopes we could sit down and discuss it when the dust settled."

"She never read your letter."

"Why not?"

Buck spun on him. "Because she told the nurse to shred it. You abandoned her in her hour of need and then you were going to hit her with a double whammy by defending yourself in a letter. Is that the gist of it?"

"It was more complicated than that. I lost my wife to cancer. I watched the woman I loved die. I felt like I was watching it again and it tore me in half. But I made a mistake. My letter was an apology, too."

Buck wiped his forehead with the back of his hand. "I'm really sorry about your wife and what you went through. But son, if you're not strong enough for Delta now, you never will be. This can come back again. What will you do if you two are together and it does? Walk away? You did what that weasel ex-husband of hers did. You left when she needed you most."

Garrett collapsed against the stall. "How could I have forgotten about him?" He'd been so wrapped up in his past colliding with the present, he'd completely disregarded her past. No wonder she'd shredded the letter. "I need to talk to her. Better yet, I need to see her. I need to do this in person."

"Not if you're going to break her heart again." Buck shook his head.

"I don't want to break it. I want to win it." Garrett held his ground. Something he should have done last week. "I regret what I did to Delta. I thought I was doing the right thing by protecting my kids from getting hurt again, but they're more hurt without her. They love Delta. And so do I. I just wish I had realized it sooner. I don't even know how she's doing because no one will tell me."

"She's much better. She wanted to work today but I told her to take it easy at home for another day or two. I'm going to stay with her for the next week, just to make sure she's okay."

Garrett wiped away a tear at the news. "I'm glad she's feeling better. Do you think I could see her?"

Buck tugged at the collar of his shirt. "It's going to take a lot more than an apology to get her attention. You need to come up with something big to win her back, because, son, you devastated her."

Something big…he knew just what to do and who to call. Come tomorrow afternoon, he'd change her mind. He refused to believe this was the end for them. He had to try or else he'd live the rest of his life in regret.

"Sir, I have an idea, but I'll need your help to pull it off."

"WHERE ARE YOU taking me?" Delta fidgeted. She preferred being the one in control, the one making the decisions. "I don't make a good passenger. I'm used to driving everywhere."

"You're going to have to get over that real quick." Her father chuckled.

"What's that supposed to mean?"

He laughed as they turned off the main road. "Today you're going to sit down, shut up and hang on."

"Dad! That's kind of rude, don't you th—" She

squealed when she saw the sign. "We're going dog-sledding?"

"You're going dogsledding. I'm heading back to work."

Delta saw Garrett's SUV parked near the entrance. "Dad, what is this all about?"

"Give the man a chance to explain. He arranged this whole thing for you yesterday because he knew you've always wanted to do this. Hear him out, enjoy the ride and if at the end of the day you want me to come get you, I will. What do you say?"

Delta reached over the armrest and hugged him. "I love you, Daddy."

"I love you, too, pumpkin." Buck kissed her on the forehead. "Now, go have some fun and don't hesitate to leave Garrett in the woods if he ticks you off."

"Believe me, there won't be any hesitation." Delta swung open the passenger door and hopped onto the hard-packed snow.

"I wasn't sure if you'd come." Garrett smiled as she approached.

"If I had known you would be here, I wouldn't have. I had no idea what my dad was up to, but kudos for getting him involved. He went from wanting to castrate you to driving me to see you. I'd say that's progress."

"I'm glad you're here. There's so much I want to tell you."

"Yeah, I don't know, Garrett." Delta turned back to the parking lot but her father had already left. "I'm here. You're here. And I've always wanted to do this. So, okay."

"Really?" Garrett smiled. "Thank you, Delta."

She followed him inside the small log cabin office. "Welcome to Musher's Dog Sled Adventures," a woman greeted them. "Do you have a reservation?"

"Garrett Slade."

"Mr. Slade, I'm the one you spoke with yesterday." She slid two clipboards with forms attached to the front of them across the counter. "If you'll fill those out for me, we'll have you out and sledding shortly. It's the perfect day for it."

Delta's hand shook with excitement as she began writing her name. If she had a bucket list, this would be pretty close to the top. She knew Garrett had planned this trip for the lodge guests, but she never expected to have the opportunity to go.

A man approached them after they'd handed in the forms. "My name is Oki and I'm your musher today. Follow me to the dog yard and meet your pack." He led them out the back door. "We offer a unique sledding experience to our guests. Most places have single person sleds, meaning the musher steers while the guest rides in the sled bed. Here all our hand-made sleds are built for three. One of you will ride up front in the bed and the other will stand on the runners behind me. Whoever's standing will experience what it's like to drive the team since you'll be helping me steer through the twists and turns of the trail."

"I'm riding in the bed." She peeked inside the nylon wrapped enclosure. Fleecy blankets lined the interior, inviting her to sink into its depths. While Oki explained how to drive and steer the sled to Garrett, she admired the team of eight dogs. She'd always assumed sled dogs were huskies or malamutes. But they had Samoyeds and

Newfoundlands, among some other breeds she didn't recognize.

"Are we ready to ride?"

"Oh, yeah." Delta rubbed her hands together in excitement. "Let's do this."

Oki strapped her safely into the sled bed as she nestled into the cocoon of warmth. "Everyone should have one of these in their house. I could fall asleep here."

"Mush!" Oki called as the sled began to move down the trail. The ride was a little bumpy at first, but once the dogs began to run, it smoothed out.

They crested a small hill and gained even more speed. Delta lifted her arms as if she were riding on a roller coaster. "Yay!" This was living. This would get her through chemotherapy this upcoming weekend. Nothing would take her down.

"How are you doing?" An hour later they were sipping hot chocolate and eating cookies while they watched Oki unhook the first team of dogs and connect the next one.

"I feel like I just ran a marathon and back. That was one of the most exhilarating things I've ever experienced."

"I'm glad you had a good time."

"Good time?" She threw her head back and laughed. "That was one of the best times of my life. This is going to sound strange, but even though I was wrapped tight in that sled bed, there was a sense of freedom, of allowing the dogs to lead us. And I know Oki was doing the driving, but from my vantage point, it was all dogs. Outside of work, I haven't had an outdoor adventure in…"

She blew out a breath. "At least a year. I've been busy ever since I moved to Saddle Ridge. This was special. This meant something. I'm so glad I got to experience this. Thank you."

Garrett understood how much freedom meant to a cancer patient regardless of their prognosis. He'd met many survivors during Rebecca's chemo treatments. Some had resigned to the disease and were tired of fighting, while others sought that freedom as if it were the last drop of water on earth. Delta was a fighter. He realized that more and more every day. Not just in her will to beat cancer, but in her fearless demeanor. He saw a renewed fire in her. When she had first come back from Missoula, it hadn't been there. That had scared him and had probably contributed to his panic over the situation.

The third anniversary of Rebecca's death had come and gone without any fanfare, mostly due to the launch of the Valentine's retreat. He had been aware of the day from the moment he opened his eyes that morning, but though it still hurt to remember her, this year the weight that had sat on his chest was no longer there. It had also given him the strength and courage to remove his wedding ring. It had been time.

"I read your letter."

"What?" Garrett's gaze met hers. "I thought you asked a nurse to destroy it."

"I did, but she slipped it in my bag and I found it last night. I guess she didn't have the heart to do it."

"Delta, I love you and I never should have reacted that way." Garrett reached for her hand only for her to pull away.

"Believe it or not, I love you, too." The pain reflecting in her eyes betrayed the sweet smile that graced her lips. "And despite my anger, I understood why you did it. After reading your letter I understand it even more. It doesn't make it hurt any less. A part of me forgives you. You lived through a terrible tragedy and our night together triggered horrible memories. I get all of that. But I'm sorry, Garrett. I can't risk those memories returning every time we share a tender moment or you see me without my hair. My body can't handle that stress right now."

Garrett's heart froze midbeat. He wanted to shout from the top of a mountain that she loved him. Those three words meant the world to him. But it wasn't enough for her to take him back. That ache was so deep and so raw he couldn't see the other side. Delta was a once-in-a-lifetime chance. And it was over. It was truly over.

DELTA ALLOWED GARRETT to drive her home and then she spent the next four hours curled up with a tissue box in one hand and Jake in the other. Her father was still working, allowing her the time to grieve for the relationship she hadn't thought she wanted.

Garrett had told her he loved her. It was the most magical phrase on earth and he'd said it to her…*her*! As light as it made her feel, she was terrified to trust her heart to him again. But she wanted to. She wanted to be the strong woman that he deserved…that the kids deserved. She just didn't know how.

Her phone rang and she was grateful for the distraction from her thoughts. The number was unfamiliar.

"Hello?"

"Hi, Delta. It's Emma. I hope I'm not calling at a bad time."

Delta forced a laugh. "Your timing couldn't be more perfect."

"I never had the opportunity to thank you for all the work you did on the Valentine's retreat."

"You're welcome. I wish I could have done more. I got a little sidelined."

"I heard. That's one of the reasons why I'm calling."

"One of?" A part of her wished she was calling on Garrett's behalf because if he asked her to give him a second chance again, she might be tempted to say yes.

"I'm calling for several reasons. To thank you and to tell you that regardless of how things end up between you and Garrett, if you ever need anything, please don't hesitate to call me. I know you have Dylan's number, but I wanted you to have mine. I know how difficult it is living away from family."

"Thank you. That's very sweet of you." Delta sniffled. "I wish things had been different."

"Maybe sometime down the road you two can try again."

"Maybe." Delta choked back a sob.

"Before I almost forget, we have a full crew coming in tonight around midnight to help us set up for Valentine's Day tomorrow. I know it's a late hour, but I wondered if you'd want to stop in and see what all your hard work looks like. Unless you want to come over now and see half of it. At midnight, you'll actually get to sample some of the food."

"Um." Delta chewed on her bottom lip. She was curious to see if her ideas looked as beautiful in person as they had on paper. And maybe she would run into Garrett and they could talk again. "I'd like that. I'll see you at midnight."

"Great, I'll see you then."

Delta dried her eyes and hopped off the couch. Midnight was only six hours away and she needed to de-snot and de-puff herself by then.

DELTA PULLED IN front of the Silver Bells Lodge at five minutes to twelve. She had expected to see trucks or more cars in the parking lot, but instead she was shrouded in silence. Then again, maybe the crews had parked around back closer to the kitchen. It made more sense.

She pushed open the doors and stepped onto a red runner strewn with white rose petals. The two-story entrance glistened in delicate twinkling lights, giving it an ethereal, fairy-tale feeling.

"Hello?" she called out, careful not to wake the guests. Guests she expected to be milling around. It was midnight and this was a couples-only retreat. She figured they would be partying into the early hours of the morning. Where was everyone?

She followed the red runner toward the great room, stopping to admire the floral arrangements she had chosen along the way. She wondered whose idea the runner had been, because it was very romantic and wedding chapel-like.

And that was when she saw them, standing at the end of the runner. Garrett, Kacey and Bryce, each holding a white long-stem rose. Tears sprang to her eyes as she quickly walked toward them. She had never been happier to see anyone in her life. This was what she wanted. They were what she wanted. She'd been a fool for ever denying herself that love.

"Did you do all this?" she asked Garrett.

"I had a little help from, well, quite a few people." He nervously laughed.

"There aren't any crews coming in tonight, are there?"

"Nope." He shook his head. "And Dylan took all the guests on a midnight snowcat tour, giving us the place to ourselves for a little while. I needed to get your attention somehow."

"You definitely have it."

"We brought you flowers." Kacey handed Delta her rose.

"Thank you, sweetie." She ran the back of her hand over Kacey's cheek. "You look so beautiful in your red dress." She turned to Bryce and accepted his rose. "And you are so handsome, little man."

"Delta?" Kacey began. "Will you ever forgive me for what happened at your house the other day?"

Delta knelt on the floor and pulled the girl into her embrace. "There is nothing to forgive, sweetheart. I know you were scared."

Garrett offered her his hand and helped her stand. "Delta, I love you. The three of us love you. Our lives are happier and fuller with you in them. We'd like to know if—"

"You'll marry us." Bryce squeezed between Kacey and Delta.

"What?" Delta looked to Garrett for confirmation.

"I was supposed to ask that question, but yes, Delta, will you marry us?"

"Please say yes." Kacey clasped her hands in front of her. "It's my birthday next week and having you for my mommy would be the best gift ever."

"How could I possibly say no to an offer like that?" Delta enveloped the girl in a hug. "I would love to be your mommy." She lifted her gaze to Garrett's. "And I would love to be your wife."

* * * * *

If you loved this novel, don't miss the next book in Amanda Renee's SADDLE RIDGE, MONTANA, *series, available May 2018!*

And check out the previous books in the series:
THE LAWMAN'S REBEL BRIDE
A SNOWBOUND COWBOY CHRISTMAS
Available now from Mills & Boon!

MILLS & BOON®

A sneak peek at next month's titles...

MILLS & BOON®

Coming next month

THE SPANISH MILLIONAIRE'S
RUNAWAY BRIDE
Susan Meier

She laughed again. "I can't even figure out how to explain running from my wedding. It's not as if I was such a great prize myself."

"You are a great prize." The words came out soft and filled with regret that her dad had skewed the way she saw herself.

She stopped at her door, but she didn't use her key card to open it. She glanced at Riccardo, her pale pink face illuminated by the light beside her door. "I'm a twenty-five-year-old woman who doesn't know who she is."

"You have to know you're beautiful."

She caught his gaze. Her long black lashes blinked over sad blue eyes. "Physical things fade."

"You're pretty in here," he countered, touching her chest just above the soft swell of her breasts. "When you're sixty, eighty, a hundred, you'll still be compassionate."

She shook her head. "You don't know that. We just met. Aside from the fact that I ran from my wedding and my dad's a bit of a control freak, you don't know much of anything about me."

Silence hung between them as they stared into each other's eyes. The warmth in her big blue orbs touched his heart, but the lift of her lips sparked a small fire in his belly. Everything male inside him awoke. The urge to kiss her tumbled through him.

He should have turned, walked the few steps to his own room and gone inside. Gotten away from her. Instead, he stayed right where he was.

Continue reading
THE SPANISH MILLIONARE'S
RUNAWAY BRIDE
Susan Meier

Available next month
www.millsandboon.co.uk

LET'S TALK
Romance

For exclusive extracts, competitions
and special offers, find us online:

f facebook.com/millsandboon

◎ @millsandboonuk

𝕐 @millsandboon

Or get in touch on 0844 844 1351*

For all the latest titles coming soon, visit
millsandboon.co.uk/nextmonth